THE NOCTURNALS

Book Three
The Fallen Star

Tracey Hecht

Fabled Films Press
New York

Published by Fabled Films LLC, New York

ISBN: 978-1-944020-05-7

Library of Congress Control Number: 2016961602

First Edition: May 2017

1 3 5 7 9 10 8 6 4 2

Cover Designed by SJI Associates
Interior Book Design by Notion Studio
Typeset in Stemple Garamond, Mrs. Ant and Pacific Northwest
Printed by Everbest in China

FABLED FILMS PRESS
NEW YORK CITY
www.fabledfilms.com

For information on bulk purchases for promotional use please contact Consortium Book Sales & Distribution Sales department at ingrampublishersvcs@ingramcontent.com or 1-866-400-5351

From the paws of
Rumur Dowling
For Carol, Jessica, and Ideal
But not without Tracey and Sarah

Book Three
The Fallen Star

Chapter One
SHOOTING STARS

"Oh goodness, there goes another one! And another and another!" Tobin cried. The pangolin's eyes grew wide as he pointed up into the night sky. His scales covered his body like the leaves of an artichoke, and now they quivered with excitement.

"I've never seen so many shooting stars!" He eagerly pointed them out to his friends, Bismark, a sugar glider, and Dawn, a red fox, who sat on either side of him. Perched on a low, sturdy branch of Bismark's pomelo tree, they had a perfect view of the streaks of light darting across the sky.

"Ah, yes, the heavens are ablaze!" Bismark leaned in toward the fox. "Though nothing rivals the flame of our true love—isn't that right, *mon amour*?" The sugar glider, who resembled a squirrel with his dark round eyes, long furry tail, and small limbs, gave the fox a quick wink.

"The sky does appear quite curious this evening," Dawn replied, ignoring her small friend.

Following the fox's gaze, Bismark and Tobin watched three more stars zip through the sky, tails of fire trailing in their wake. Each star briefly cast the shadowy treetops throughout the forest in a soft, blue, glittering light.

"Oh my," Tobin said, clasping his claws together. "They just keep coming! Have you ever seen so many shooting stars at once?"

Dawn watched another set of stars flash through the night like a school of silver minnows swimming in a dark pond. Her eyes flared with their reflection. The sky was indeed fascinating tonight.

"It's the most beautiful, brilliant sky I've ever seen!" Tobin added.

"Beautiful, yes, but brilliant? Not quite."

10

Bismark stood up on his short, scrawny legs. "For true brilliance, *mi amigo*, look no further than the star of the stars, the flame of the fire, the–"

"Bismark–" Dawn interrupted.

"–spectacle of the spectacular!" Bismark finished proudly, and flung out his arms so that his flaps, the stretchy skin connecting his four limbs, billowed in the breeze. Then, with a loud whoop, the glider launched from his perch, letting the warm nighttime air lift him. With the air ballooning beneath his flaps, he sailed to another branch of his pomelo tree with ease.

"And that, *mes amis*, is the true shooting star of the valley!" Bismark lowered his head with a bow.

Tobin clapped his long, taloned claws together and giggled with delight.

Dawn raised an eyebrow, but her lips curved into a small smile. Then she returned her gaze to the sky, just in time to watch another smattering of shooting stars crisscross above.

"Well then," continued Bismark, lowering his arms and surveying the branches overhead. "If my flaps don't catch your fancy, *mon amour*, perhaps my fruit will. What's a star show without a little snack, anyway? Who's up for a pomelo?"

"Oh goodness," said Tobin. The bulky belly

of his anteater-like body rumbled at the thought. "A pomelo would be lovely."

"Yes, yes, scaly one. We know you're always hungry!" Bismark reached for one of the glistening, golden-green citrus fruits hanging heavily from the branch above his head and plucked it with a snap. "And for you, *mi bella*? A little bit of sugar for my sweet?"

Dawn nodded, but her amber eyes remained fixed on the stars above.

The glider scurried across the branch and around the tree trunk to his friends, a plump grapefruit-like pomelo in hand. "Your wish is my command!"

With a slick swish of his claws, Bismark split the pomelo open and sliced it into thirds. Its skin—coral, emerald, and gold—unfurled to reveal a treasure of ruby-red wedges within. "*Voilà*!" he exclaimed. "Here it is!"

"Oh goodness, this one looks delicious," said Tobin. The pangolin uncurled his long, pink tongue. It was so long, in fact, that he coiled it inside his stomach when he wasn't using it. But now that it was exposed and outstretched, he eagerly used it to lap at his share of the fruit.

"Would you expect anything less, *muchacho*?" said Bismark. His face shone with the sticky pulp of his own piece, which he eagerly devoured. "Everyone knows my tree grows the sweetest, tastiest pomelos in the valley."

As the three friends chewed contentedly, they watched the streaks of light from the shooting stars gradually dim. The moon began to fade with the approach of sunrise. After a lone shooting star vanished across the horizon, Dawn rose to her feet.

"That seems to have been the last of them," she said. The fox swallowed her final piece of pomelo and stretched her willowy limbs. "Perhaps it's time for bed."

Bismark leaped to his feet. "My thoughts exactly, *chérie*!" he said, scrambling to her side. "A glider this *grandissimo* needs his beauty rest, after all. Allow me to walk with you to your lovely home."

Tobin yawned, his eyelids drooping. Like his two friends, the pangolin was nocturnal: asleep by day, awake by night. But as he started to rise, something twinkling in the distance caught his attention.

"Oh goodness, wait! There's one more," he cried, pointing to the horizon. Indeed, another shooting star had appeared. Only this one seemed different. It was brighter—much, much brighter—than the others. As it streaked across the sky, it seemed as if the entire valley was suddenly illuminated by a second, more dazzling moon.

13

"Ooh! Let's all make a wish on this one—the brightest of them all," said the pangolin. "I wish…" His scaly brow furrowed. "I wish that we could have as many pomelos as we could ever eat!"

"*Amigo*! Has all that sugar gone to your skull?" Bismark scrambled higher into his tree to watch the star's fiery flight. "Everyone knows that if you say your wish aloud, it won't come true. Of course, it goes without saying what *I* wish for—isn't that right, *mi bella*?" Bismark said, returning to Dawn with his small hand on his heart.

But the fox said nothing in response. Instead, her amber eyes narrowed as she tracked this final star shooting across the southern sky. This one wasn't fading away like the others. No—this one looked like it was growing brighter. And brighter. And brighter still.

"Bismark, Tobin…" Dawn's voice carried an air of alarm.

"Yes, what is it my sweet? Has the moment arrived for us finally to declare our true feelings? Has this brilliant blaze in the sky sparked the flame of love in your heart?" Bismark's voice trailed off. "Hmm, this star sure is taking its sweet time falling…and falling… and falling…"

The sugar glider blinked and rubbed his eyes.

The star's flame was now so bright, he could hardly focus on it.

Increasing in speed, the shooting star dipped lower and lower.

Tobin's mouth dropped open. "D-Dawn? What's going on?" The frightened pangolin's voice came out in a whisper.

The fox stared in disbelief. The star was traveling closer and closer. It was heading right toward them!

"Great Scott! It's coming for me!" Bismark cried.

"Everyone, hold on!" commanded the fox.

The three friends dug their claws into the tree bark and ducked as a blinding ball of light shot overhead. It sizzled and buzzed and hissed as it traveled through the sky in a low arc. Its fiery blaze stunned their eyes and forced them to crouch for cover.

And then, just as fast, all went silent, and the sky darkened.

After a tense moment, the trio slowly gazed up.

Bismark rubbed his big brown eyes. "Phew! That was a close one. But nothing *I* was scared of, of course. Just a—"

BAM!

Without warning, a massive explosion rippled through the valley with a deafening roar. The tops of the trees waved violently in a huge blast of wind. Entire branches of pomelos splintered off and tumbled to the ground, their leaves twisting and turning in the whirling, swirling air.

"*Mon dieu*!" Bismark clung to Dawn's leg in terror.

The earth shook, boulders rattled and jumped, and Bismark's tree lurched, hurling the three from their perches. Tobin and Dawn dropped straight to the forest floor with heavy, headfirst thuds. Bismark tried to hold fast to his branch, but it snapped off in his claws. With a crack, he was sent hurtling high into the air, like a stone flung from a slingshot.

"This calls for the flaps!" the glider cried, desperately stretching his limbs to catch a gust of wind. But the wild, whistling air blew his flaps inside out, and the next thing he knew, he was spiraling down, down, down to the earth in a rain of falling pomelos and leaves.

Chapter Two
ALL ALONE

"Oomph!"

Tobin groaned. Then he peeled his sensitive eyes open and cringed. The pangolin had taken quite a nasty tumble. His skull was throbbing, and his limbs felt stiff and sore as he gingerly uncurled his body. He had rolled into a tight ball before hitting the ground—this was the position he took whenever he felt frightened or threatened. But now he sat upright, taking a deep breath and scanning his surroundings nervously.

"Dawn? Bismark?" he called into the darkness.

Tobin looked in every direction but saw only piles of fallen branches and brush. Three nearby trees had been uprooted whole, and several large boulders had tumbled forward, careening into each other. *What happened?* the pangolin wondered, rubbing his head, his thoughts cloudy. Then he remembered: the falling star! He frantically looked to the sky.

But now, all seemed calm. The full moon was hanging serenely above the forest. The stars that circled it were twinkling, not falling. Tobin exhaled.

"Oh goodness," he murmured with relief. But then he realized that the moon was hanging high in the sky, even though it had been nearly sunup before the fallen star had crashed to earth. That meant the whole day had passed! Had he really been unconscious that long? The pangolin's heart started to race.

"Dawn? Bismark?" he called out again, this time with more urgency. There was no sign of his friends. He dug at the piles of debris, searching for them. Rocks, clods of dirt, and grass shot out behind him. "Oh goodness! Where is everyone?" he whimpered as he moved among the rubble.

"Tobin?" a voice called out.

The pangolin froze. Someone was burrowing

out of a pile of leaves and branches near one of the fallen trees. Someone with tawny fur and a familiar, white-tipped tail.

"Dawn!" he cried. The pangolin raced over to help free his friend. Then he brushed the leaves off her coat.

Dawn shook the remaining leaves from her limbs. She took note of the moonlight and narrowed her eyes. "An entire day has passed, but we are lucky to be unharmed." Then, noticing the sugar glider's absence, her voice tightened. "Tobin, where is Bismark?"

Dawn and Tobin gazed up to search the heights of Bismark's pomelo tree. Its branches, normally covered with thick leaves and heavy fruit, were almost entirely bare. There was no sign of the glider anywhere.

"Oh goodness!" cried Tobin.

Dawn quickly began to clear the earth, flinging aside the branches and pomelos that littered the forest floor. Tobin, meanwhile, lowered his keen snout to the ground, nostrils flaring. He could track almost anything with his superior sense of smell.

"Bismark! Where are you?" he called as he sniffed. The pangolin gulped. Why wasn't Bismark answering? Where was the glider's boisterous voice? His familiar musk? Tobin furiously inhaled the scents along the earth, searching for a sign of his friend.

The pangolin poked his snout into a pile of broken, spear-like sticks. Their jagged ends scratched his nose. "Oh!" he muttered, but then he paused. A whiff of damp fur played over his nostrils. His eyes widened.

"Dawn!" he cried.

The fox sprinted over at once. She grasped the sharp branches in her jaws and cracked them in half while Tobin shoveled branches and dirt behind them. Then, together, they lifted up one last clawful of leaves, and there he was: Bismark, flaps splayed flat, eyes clamped shut, and an angry welt protruding from the bald spot in the center of his head.

"Oh dear!" Tobin cried, bending low toward his friend. "Bismark? Bismark? Wake up!"

The pangolin's snout was nearly touching the glider's tiny face. "Bismark, can you hear me?" he asked. After a moment Tobin straightened and looked at the fox, fear welling in his eyes. "Dawn! He's not answering! Is Bismark...? Is he...?" Tobin swallowed hard. He tried to speak, but he could not utter the rest.

Chapter Three
MIDNIGHT-BLUE CAPES

Dawn gently moved Tobin aside. Then she turned to Bismark and studied him with a steady gaze. The moment seemed to last for ages, but finally, she relaxed. Bismark's chest was rising and falling, ever so slightly. The movement was nearly invisible to most, but not to the fox's keen eyesight.

"He's alive," she sighed as she relaxed onto her rear haunches. She looked at the bare pomelo tree branches overhead. "It's a long drop from up there, but his flaps likely softened his fall."

Tobin eagerly leaned in close to his friend, trying to detect the glider's breathing for himself.

Suddenly, Bismark's eyelids fluttered. "Ah, *mi bella* Dawn, is that you?" he mumbled. "Your voice is moonlit music to my tired ears. Come, my sweet *señorita*, lean in, let our hearts beat as one." He puckered his small lips for a kiss.

"Oh goodness, Bismark!" said Tobin, quickly pulling away.

The sugar glider's eyes shot open. "Ack! *Amigo*, is that you?" Bismark leaped to his feet with sudden, renewed strength and frantically wiped his mouth with his flaps. "Irresistible as I may be, *mon ami*, you must learn to control yourself! Tame those emotions! Dawn is the one I love! He dusted himself off and stood up tall.

"Oh Bismark, you're all right!" Tobin exclaimed, enjoying his friend's familiar banter.

The sugar glider paused. He stared at the piles of sticks, rocks, and ruin. Pomelos from his tree lay scattered all about: bruised orbs of greenish-gold against piles of brown dirt and rubble.

"*Uno momento*! Not so fast! I may *look* all right, but I most certainly am not!" Bismark exclaimed. "Look at what has become of the bounty of my tree!" He lifted a smushed pomelo in his paw.

"Oh, Bismark, don't worry!" Tobin foraged about frantically and finally located a single, unharmed fruit. "They're not all bad. And we're lucky the shooting star didn't land right on top of us!"

"Yes, we were lucky...." Dawn said, voice trailing off. The falling star hit the valley the night before—that much was clear. But if Bismark's entire tree had lost all its fruit here, how bad was the damage elsewhere?

"Others might not have been as fortunate as we were," she said. "We must find the star at once and see if anyone has been hurt."

"*Mon dieu*, that's right! The fallen star!" Bismark's gaze shot upward to the dark sky above as he remembered the incidents of the previous night. The moon reflected in his bulbous brown eyes, and he rubbed his paws together. "*Mi amore*, our very own piece of the heavens has descended. Now it is waiting in the forest for us to claim it!"

The sugar glider scurried to the fox. "Don't you realize what this means?" he continued. "The night sky has sent us a symbol of our love! Haven't I always told you I'd bring you the moon, the stars, the heavens? Yes, we must brave this destruction and go find it at once. But first—"

The glider put one finger up to signal his friends to wait. Then he scurried to a hollow in the trunk of his tree. There, he retrieved a midnight-blue snakeskin cape and tied it around his neck. "This calls for the Nocturnal Brigade!"

In the night world of the valley, the Nocturnal Brigade was the name that the three friends were known by. Bold in adventure and brave in challenge, they came to the rescue of creatures in danger or in need of their help.

Bismark gestured toward Dawn and Tobin and urged them to follow. "Come on, *amigos*, we cannot venture forth without our proper attire!"

Tobin gathered his cape and Dawn's as well. He grinned as he secured his around his neck.

"The Nocturnal Brigade is back at it!" Bismark exclaimed, stretching an arm toward the fox. "Shall we, *mon amour*?"

Dawn draped her cape around her neck. "Yes, we must go see if anyone needs our help." The fox took one final glance at the fallen trees and split branches around them. "I hope we're not too late."

Chapter Four
THE FALLEN STAR

"Keep...churning...those paws...*mes amis!*" Bismark coughed his way through the thick, dusty air. The Brigade was moving through the forest, heading in the direction of the fallen star. Dawn and Tobin raced along the ground while Bismark soared up above, flinging his small body through the treetops.

"Oh dear." Tobin coughed, too. The pangolin was pushing his stout legs to their limit, but the air around him grew dustier and dustier. It was getting harder to breathe, and it was becoming more difficult to see—the pangolin's already fuzzy vision had begun to blur, and his eyes filled with tears.

Tobin lifted his snout. "Ah-choo!" he sneezed. A burning, metallic reek stung his nose. There was something gritty and hot hanging in the haze. "Dawn? Bismark? Do you feel that, too?"

Bismark had landed on the peak of a tall elm tree, where he shielded his eyes with a flap. From his perch, he could see a huge tower of dust billowing from the south. It was gradually spreading throughout the entire valley.

"*Mon dieu*," he muttered. "All this gunk on my lustrous coat!" He sailed a few tree lengths ahead. The closer he drew toward the fallen star, the less foliage there was in the tree tops. And fewer leaves meant less shelter from the clouds of dust rapidly approaching.

"I'm blinder than a bat up here." Bismark spat. "This will never do." Spreading his flaps out wide, he let himself float to the ground in front of his friends. "Bad news, *amigos*! Thick clouds are rolling in. I can hardly see my own flaps up there. We must abandon the mission!"

"Bismark, animals could be hurt," Dawn said as she leaped over a fallen log. "We must hurry."

Scrambling alongside his friends, Tobin tried

his best to feel his way through the swirling sand. "Oh goodness, I can hardly see a thing!" he said. "And that smell...it's getting worse!" His sensitive snout was beginning to burn.

"*Mon dieu*, indeed it is! It's stinking like a boar's backside!" Bismark said with a retch.

"Hmm, it doesn't smell quite like that, Bismark," Tobin said, frowning. He tested the air with his snout. "It's more like...like..." He shut his eyes to focus on the odor. He tottered forward, nose titled high in the air. "Like something's on fire–"

"Tobin, look out!" Dawn suddenly shouted.

The pangolin's eyes shot open, but it was too late. His claws had caught on a fallen branch, and he flipped right over the ledge of an unexpected drop. He quickly curled into his protective ball of armor and rolled down the slope like a runaway pinecone. Faster and faster he went as he careened away from his friends.

"*Dios mio*, Señor Scales! Look at you go!" Bismark cried. "Wait for us, oh circular one! We were not made to bounce and bowl like you!" The glider spread his flaps and glided down the slope after Tobin. Dawn picked up her pace as quickly as she could.

"Oof! Ow! Ouch!" the pangolin grunted as he bounded down the hillside. To protect himself, he tucked in his limbs, creating an even tighter ball, but this only made him roll faster.

"Slow down, *muchacho*! I am supposed to be the fleetest-of-flaps around here!" Bismark shouted. The glider was skimming the surface of the ground at top speed, landing every so often to sprint a few steps and then take off once more. Dawn followed close behind in a blur of amber fur.

"Tobin, stop! Use your claws!" she yelled.

"Oh goodness, I'm trying!" the pangolin called back. He jammed his claws into the earth, but he was tumbling too rapidly to bring himself to a halt. Bouncing off a bump, Tobin launched into the air. For a brief moment, his round body seemed to hover weightlessly, concealing the full moon in a total eclipse.

"Your arms, *mi amigo*, flap your arms! Bismark cried. "Oh *mon dieu*, he's going to crash like the falling star! This is it, the end, the final good-bye. *Hasta luego*, oh scaly one!"

"Tobin!" Dawn shouted. "Reach for me!" The fox leaped through the air with all her strength and caught the pangolin's bulky body with her front legs. Tobin's stumpy arms wrapped around her neck as she guided him to the ground with a thump, her body softening his fall.

"Oh *fantastico*! *Mi amore, mi amigo*, what form, what grace, what *panache*!" The sugar glider applauded. He skidded to a dusty halt next to his friends. "But I must ask, my love, where was that saving embrace last night, when the one hurtling to the ground was *moi*?"

Tobin, meanwhile, examined his scales for scratches. He steadied his legs and looked up at the steep ledge where he had tripped and taken flight. "I don't remember there being a cliff in this part of the valley."

Dawn was thinking the same thing. Her eyes strained through the clouds of dry earth that the three had kicked up in their descent. Where were they? All she could tell was that they had dropped somewhere far below the normal level of the forest floor. But how was that possible?

Then, suddenly, Dawn detected something in the dusty dark, and her eyes flickered with understanding. "That was no cliff," she said.

There was a brief pause. Tobin and Bismark stared at her blankly.

"My lady, maybe your fall to the earth last night didn't go as smoothly as I thought," Bismark said, scratching his chin. "Trust me, we sugar gliders know all about the dangerous drops of the earth. That one, my lady, is *absolutamente* a cliff."

"No, Bismark," she replied coolly. "It's a crater! And—look! That's what we've been searching for."

The fox gestured into the gloom. The dust had settled around the Brigade, and as the air cleared a dark shape was slowly materializing out of the shadows. The trio watched the dim form in awe. Then, at last, a moonbeam glinted off its surface, bringing it into focus: it was the fallen star!

Tobin gasped.

"Way to go, *pangolino*! Your tuck-and-roll brought us right to it! That and the radiant rescue from my lady," said Bismark, nudging the fox's haunches.

The three friends stared up at the strange, foreign object. It was a large, dark mass, roughly the size and shape of a hippopotamus. Except for a jagged crack across the front, it was as smooth and black as volcanic glass.

"So this is what a fallen star looks like? A giant rock? A stone from the sky?" Bismark asked, stepping toward the star to peek inside its fracture. "Where's all the light? The heat? The shining brilliance of the stars? All this one's got is a little crack.... Too dark to see inside, though . . ."

"Don't get too close," Dawn warned. From a few paw's lengths away, the fox studied the black stony object. "When a star falls from above and crashes to Earth, it takes this form. I've heard that it is called a meteorite." She began circling the stone.

"Oh goodness, it still smells like it's on fire!" Tobin noted, his nose twitching.

"It burned scars into the earth," Dawn noted. "And look, it also left these strange mounds of dirt…." Her voice trailed off, and she frowned.

The glider stepped back from the stone's crevice and checked the ground beneath his feet. Dawn was right—the meteorite was surrounded by little clods of dirt, each one with a tiny hole in the middle.

"Never fear, *mon amour*! Just a bit of stardust," he said, poking at one of the mounds. It crumbled at his touch. "*Blech*! Kind of grimy, actually."

The fox inspected the piles around her paws. They appeared to be freshly dug. "Careful what you touch," she said.

While the sugar glider flicked bits of dirt from his claws, Tobin also took a closer look at the fallen star and the ground surrounding it. "What could have made all these mounds?" he murmured. The pangolin turned to Dawn.

She shifted her jaw uneasily.

"Not much could have survived the meteorite's

impact," she mused. "Insects, perhaps. Or maybe some kind of—"

Tap tap tap.

The fox's mouth snapped shut.

Tap tap tap.

The noise was coming from the stone.

Tap tap tap.

"*Mon dieu!*" Bismark gulped, backing away. "The fallen star is alive!"

Chapter Five
THE INVASION

Tap tap tap.

Tap tap tap.

Dawn took a cautious step forward. As she approached, the mysterious tapping grew louder. More insistent.

Tap tap tap!

Tap tap tap!

"My lady, look out! That hunk of rock is not

to be trusted!" Bismark cried, hiding behind Tobin's armored tail.

Dawn peered at the stone. "Who's there?" she called.

"*Dios mio*! Something's moving!" The sugar glider pointed to a figure emerging from behind the star.

The Brigade stepped back in shock. A strange animal was slowly rising from the shadows. Tobin gasped as its two bony hands came into view, each one sporting a fourth finger that was nearly twice as long as all the others. Then he raised his eyes to take in the rest of the creature: two leathery ears, a pair of orange eyes, a wrinkled face, and a furry body with a thick, bushy tail. With its rodent-like fangs, grimy fur, and massive, fiery eyes, it looked like a small monkey crossed with a swamp rat.

"*Mon dieu*! It's the monster of the fallen star!" Bismark cried. "Stand back, foul beast! Stay away, filthy fiend! Oh heaven above, you have sent one miserable *muchacha* down to us!"

"Um, hello?" the much more polite pangolin said, nudging Bismark with his snout. Still, Tobin had to admit—the newcomer's appearance was startling. He had never seen anything like it.

"By the stars! Look at those fingers! That scowl!

That drool!" Bismark continued. "I want to look away, but I cannot!"

"Be quiet, Bismark," Dawn scolded. "She's an aye-aye, the rarest type of lemur in the valley. I've heard them described, but I've never actually seen one before."

"Do not be *ridiculo*, my love! Everyone knows that lemurs are primates of soft fuzz and sweet fur!" the sugar glider cried. "This one looks like she was born in a prickle bush!"

"Enough, Bismark," Dawn said. She turned to the aye-aye. "Forgive us," she began. "We've come to see if anyone was hurt by the star. I am Dawn, and this is Bismark and Tobin. We are the Nocturnal Brigade."

"What is your name?" Tobin offered shyly.

The aye-aye did not answer. Instead, she began to climb the meteorite. When she reached its top, she turned to the trio, staring with her large eyes. Then she used her elongated fourth finger to tap against the stone.

Tap tap tap.

"*Mon dieu*, that miserable *muchacha's* finger is as long as your tongue, amigo!" Bismark whispered, poking the pangolin's flanks. The glider's gaze moved to the sharp tips of the aye-aye's grimy nails, and he shuddered.

"Hey! Wait just a *momento*," he cried. "I think I'm on to something! Listen up, Madame Monstruoso.

Was it you who dug these holes in the soil? Quick, someone check those fingers for dirt!"

"Oh goodness, Bismark! Give her a chance to speak," Tobin whispered to his friend.

But despite his good intentions, the pangolin felt a surge of dread as the aye-aye turned her harsh gaze on him. Perched upon the stone, she looked like some kind of hairy vulture at roost. Finally, she opened her mouth and wheezed a shallow cough.

"A stone, a star-stone, fallen from the sky! It has come, but it did not come alone," she said. Her raspy voice echoed faintly off the smooth meteorite. "Aye-Aye Iris has seen them. The mounds have been made. The poison has been set. The creatures are among us. The invasion has begun!"

"Oh goodness! Poison? Creatures? Invasion!?" Tobin cried.

"*Mon dieu*!" Bismark exclaimed. "Invaders? In the valley?"

The fur on Dawn's neck stood on end, but her voice remained steady and calm. "What kind of creatures did you see?" she asked the hunched animal above her.

The aye-aye sputtered. Her shoulders heaved with each raspy breath. She wheezed and clutched her sides. But she said nothing in reply. She just continued to stare down at the Brigade. Dawn noticed that in all this time, the lemur had not blinked even once. Was something wrong with her? Was she ill? Or was she simply rattled by the fallen star?

"What evidence do you have of an invasion? Of poison?" the fox pressed, meeting the aye-aye's spellbinding stare with a steady look of her own.

But the aye-aye just clicked her tongue and licked her lips, as if detecting the scent of something ripe in the air. "They have landed," she repeated simply. "They have come. And they will destroy us all."

"For the love of all things gracious and good!" Bismark said, taking a few steps away from the aye-aye. "Who are these invaders? What do they want?"

The aye-aye opened her mouth to speak but then stopped. Her pointy ears twitched in their beds of stringy white fur.

"This is all starting to sound a little loco," Bismark continued. "I think that hair of yours might not be the only thing in need of untangling, *comprende*?"

The aye-aye hissed. Her face morphed into a grimace. "Aye-Aye Iris knows! Aye-Aye Iris knows!" She rapped her finger against the meteorite.

"Aye-Aye Iris," Dawn's voice softened to calm the distraught lemur. "Please, tell us: who are these invaders? Where are they?" Dawn's gaze swept the area, searching for intruders.

"Yes! Where are they?" echoed the sugar glider. Bismark lifted his arms and took in the surroundings with a flourish of his flaps. "*Regardez,* there is no one here but us. We are solo. *Inoccupato.* Alone!" The glider planted his hands on his hips and cleared his throat, as if he were going to continue.

The aye-aye's stare hardened, but she remained silent.

Dawn took two small steps toward her. "Iris, what do the invaders look like? What poison have they set?"

"Only Aye-Aye Iris knows!" screeched the lemur. "Aye-Aye Iris knows the secret!" She doubled over and wheezed some more.

"What secret?" Dawn prodded.

"Follow Aye-Aye Iris," the lemur said. She took a step toward the edge of the meteorite and beckoned the Brigade with her finger.

The glider recoiled. Stumbling backward, he gathered his friends toward him with his flaps. "*Mon dieu,* she's as crazy as she looks! *Muy loco,* totally mad! Who would believe such outrageous talk? She makes no sense!" he cried.

Iris's bat-like ears twitched at the sound of Bismark's mocking tone, and she let out a garbled grunt. "You don't believe Aye-Aye Iris, hmm?" She pointed her finger at the sugar glider. "Very well then, very well!"

In a movement of surprising grace, the aye-aye slid from the stone. Then, with her posture slumped, she started trekking across the crater. Her spindly limbs moved like the legs of an enormous spider as she propelled herself away from the Brigade and into the thick dust.

"Wait." Tobin glanced nervously at the strange lemur moving farther and farther away. "Shouldn't we stop her?" He turned to Dawn and Bismark. "Don't you think we should find out the secret? Just in case?"

"No! Don't be silly, *amigo*," said the glider. "She is crazy, bonkers, insane! But I do suggest we *vamanos* before Lady Loco decides to return and do something to us with those freaky fingers of hers."

And then, just as she began to recede from view, one of the lemur's long, lanky fingers emerged from the haze. She pointed it at the Brigade.

"Mark these words, sugar glider! Fox! Pangolin!" Her voice carried through the gloom. "You shall know when you see the glow. Beware the glow!" She paused dramatically. "But also know this," she continued. "Once you see it, it will be too late." Iris shook her head. Then she let out a cackle that echoed through the darkness.

The Brigade squinted into the distance after the aye-aye, but they soon lost sight of her altogether. The air hung as heavy and thick as the eerie silence that remained.

"Uh, wait! *Muchacha*! Perhaps I was a bit rash, a bit hasty. You know, distracted by those fearsome...I mean, fancy fingers of yours!" Bismark called after her.

But there was no response.

The aye-aye had disappeared.

If there was a secret to learn, the aye-aye had taken it with her.

Chapter Six
THE OMINOUS AYE-AYE

"No, my *amigos*, it is just as I suspected—there is zippo! Zero! *Zilch*!" Bismark shouted. Standing on tiptoe on top of Tobin's pointy snout, the sugar glider peered inside the fallen star's crack. "But pee-yew! Is the star stone still burning, or did that aye-aye, Iris, leave behind her stench?" He flapped himself away from the rotten fumes rising from the meteorite and landed back on the ground with a huff.

"Oh goodness, are you sure there's nothing in

there?" Tobin asked his friend. "No star creatures? No glow?"

"*Mon ami*, I assure you—the only creature near this rock was that long-fingered loony," Bismark said. "Besides, who has ever heard of such a story? Critters from the stars? Poison from the sky? A mysterious glow? Pah, I say. *Ridiculo!*"

Tobin pawed nervously at one of the small dirt piles around the fallen star. "But what about these mounds?" he asked.

Dawn slowly paced in front of the meteorite, eyeing the crater that it had created and the strange mounds that surrounded it. She stepped closer to the fallen star and was surprised to see her reflection in the stone's glossy surface. She turned to face her friends.

"The explosion, the smell, this crater—the meteorite caused these things—" she started.

"Couldn't have said it better myself, mon amour," Bismark interrupted. "Looks like we've cracked the case! Another job well done by the Nocturnal Brigade. We found the stone, though it wasn't exactly as *romantique* as I thought it would be, thanks to that cuckoo creature. But no matter. Let's head on home. Excellent work, *mes amis. Muy, muy bueno.*"

Tobin watched the fox continue to paw at the

mounds scattered around the meteor.

"But I can't explain these," Dawn finished.

"Hmm." Bismark stared into the stone. "For a hunk of cold, hard rock from outer space, this fallen star sure is attractive!" The glider flexed an arm and posed in front of the meteorite, which reflected his movements like the surface of a black, depthless sea. "*Mon dieu*, I am handsome! No wonder that creepy *cucaracha* couldn't keep her eyes off me."

The fox ignored her friend's ranting and took one last careful look around the crater. Besides the mounds in the earth, there was no sign of anything unusual or any real harm done.

She sniffed the air and pricked her ears, but nothing odd caught her attention. She frowned. Perhaps she should take the meteorite's safe landing as a good omen: truly a lucky star, after all. And in that case, Bismark was right—the Brigade had done their duty.

"Let us go. There's much to clean up in the valley," the fox said. She turned to lead her friends on the hike back up the crater's steep slope, her tail swishing as she moved.

"Oh you lady fox! I love it when you hustle and bustle," Bismark called in reply, trotting to catch up.

As the Brigade made their way back into

the forest, the sugar glider stepped alongside the trundling pangolin and extended his pointer finger with exaggeration.

"*Tap tap tap. Tap tap tap!*" he said, poking the pangolin's scales.

"Oh goodness, Bismark!" Tobin laughed nervously, glancing about with unease.

"Loosen up, *amigo*, that aye-aye was a bit bananas, yes, but nothing to be worried about."

The Brigade continued through the forest. As they neared home, the moon faded in the sky, and the first fingertips of sunrise began to creep across the horizon. Tobin yawned. It had been a very long night.

Dawn smiled at her tired friends then let out a small yawn herself. "Let's get some sleep," she suggested. The fox padded toward a fallen tree and then, using her tail, swept its loose leaves into a comfortable mound. "Cleanup can wait until nightfall when we are better rested."

"Good idea, my fair fox!" Bismark bounded toward Dawn and leaped into her pile of leaves, creating a flurry around him. "Nothing like a snuggle with my sweet!"

With a good-natured roll of her eyes, the fox scooted sideways, creating space between her and the sugar glider. Then she curled up in a crescent and allowed her eyes to close.

Tobin settled nearby and released a contented sigh. It had been an exhausting, strange night, but all was well. *A lucky star*, he thought, remembering the brilliant flash across the dark sky. And then he fell asleep.

*   *   *

Guuuurrrrgghhh.

The pangolin awoke to the sound of a loud grumble.

His eyes shot open. The sky was a rich periwinkle; he had slept straight through until dusk.

Guuuurrrrgghhh!

"*Mon dieu*," Bismark groaned, rubbing his eyes. "What is that racket? That rumble? That noise? Has another meteorite struck the earth?"

"Oh goodness." Tobin grinned bashfully. "It's just my stomach. I'm afraid I've woken up hungry."

The fox rose to her feet and smiled. "We need to check the meteorite's damage," she said. "But we'll start back at Bismark's pomelo tree, where there will be plenty of pomelos to satisfy your appetite."

"Pomelos!" cheered Tobin.

"Fallen pomelos," grunted the sugar glider.

Tobin grinned. "Yes...and someone's got to eat them before they go bad, right?" And then, with a small yelp of excitement, he hastened to a trot, leading his friends down the final stretch of path to the forest's edge. But just as soon as he reached the clearing and Bismark's pomelo tree came into view, something brought him to an abrupt halt.

"Oh goodness!" the pangolin cried. He gestured frantically at the ground. "Dawn, Bismark! Look!"

The pangolin began to tremble at the sight. Bismark's tree was surrounded by dozens and dozens of mounds of loose soil, just like the ones at the star. What's more, all the glider's fallen pomelos had been viciously torn open and savagely clawed to shreds.

Dawn remained silent, but her amber eyes widened with alarm and suspicion.

Bismark's eyes bulged. "By all that is nightly!" he screamed. "It is an attack! We have been invaded!"

Chapter Seven
SOMETHING FRUITY,
SOMETHING FOUL

Bismark sprinted around the clearing, stooping to inspect the pomelos as he ran. Each one was the same: brutally split open and drained of its succulent juice.

"My poor, *pauvres pomelos!*" the glider cried. "Taken before their time was ripe! Pinched before their prime of life! That long-fingered lemur was right: the star creatures have attacked!"

"Oh goodness!" Tobin cried nervously. "Do you really think there are invaders or star creatures?"

The fox cautiously sniffed at the mounds of dirt. The disturbed soil smelled moist. And there was something else—a tang she could not identify. A foreign odor. This scent was fresh. It couldn't have been left more than few moments ago—they'd arrived only minutes after the culprits had gone!

"Oh goodness!" the pangolin gasped again. His stomach growled loudly at the sight of all the wasted pomelos. Ruined! But as he moved about the mangled mess, the tempting scent of oozing fruit filled his nostrils. This comforting odor distracted him from all thoughts of invaders. It spoke to his stomach, calming his worried mind. The pomelos may have been mashed—but he was sure they'd still be delicious!

"Oh!" Tobin said as he tromped over to what appeared to be a perfect pomelo. He cautiously rolled the fruit over with his snout. It did have a gash in its peel, but most of its flesh was still intact. "This one still looks okay," he said quietly as he cradled it in his paws.

The pangolin's mouth watered. His stomach rumbled. He studied the cut in the greenish-yellow rind and frowned.

Not so bad, really, he convinced himself. "Perhaps I'll just try a little…." Slowly, Tobin inched open his jaw. His long tongue extended from his mouth and sank into the sweet, citrusy fruit. He lapped up a large piece of the fruit and swallowed.

"Oh!" the pangolin gasped as his mouth immediately flared with an intense burning sensation.

Dawn whipped toward him at once. "Tobin, no!" she cried. "Don't touch the fruit!"

Tobin dropped the pomelo, his tiny black eyes tearing as he sealed his mouth shut to silence his pain.

"You didn't eat any, did you?" Dawn pressed, staring at her friend's bleary eyes.

Embarrassed, Tobin shook his head no.

"Good," said the fox, relieved. "We must not touch this fruit until we know who or what attacked it."

Tobin nodded again to agree with his leader. Then he gulped. His tongue still burned—it felt as if he were sucking an ember. His stomach felt tied up in knots, and suddenly, a smelly green poof escaped from his rear. This was the spray he released, much like a skunk, whenever he felt afraid or in danger.

"*Ay, caramba*! What's with the stench, *mon ami*?" Bismark cried, holding his nose and fanning the air with his flap. "We're all a bit scared of these so-called invaders, but try to hold off on the stink! We've got enough fumes flying around here."

Tobin's mouth curled into a grimace. His legs

started to wobble, and his brow broke into a cold sweat.

"Tobin, are you all right?" Dawn asked noticing his pained frown. She put a paw on his scaly shoulder.

The pangolin's tongue burned too much to speak, so he simply whimpered and pointed at one of the pomelos.

"Oh, we know, my scaly *hermano*." Bismark sighed. "It breaks the heart. Torments the *tête*. Tortures the soul! Our beauties...lying here like wreckage!" He turned to Tobin. "Have no shame, *amigo*. This sight could make even the bravest of *hombres* cry." Bismark dabbed the corner of his eye.

Tobin nodded. The fiery sensation in his mouth was not lessening. His lips stung, and his stomach was growing hot. He needed to tell his friends what he'd done. He had to. Tobin swallowed hard, preparing to confess, but then:

"*Eurrrghhhhh*!" A loud noise ripped through the clearing.

The pangolin gasped. It sounded like a large, menacing beast...and it was coming from the bushes behind the Brigade.

"Great Scott!" wailed Bismark. "It's the invaders! They've come back for us! This is it, *amigos*! The end! *La fin*! Oh my *bella* Dawn, our time together was so short, yet so sweet—"

"*Eurrrghhhhhh!*" The noise sounded again, this time accompanied by the sound of crunching leaves underfoot.

Tobin curled into a ball. His tongue flamed and his stomach churned.

"Who goes there?" Bismark's voice wavered as he scrambled behind the fox.

Dawn shifted her weight, shoulders lowered and hind legs tensed, taking her striking position.

The sound of crunching leaves grew louder. The Brigade had company.

Chapter Eight
THE POMELO PLAGUE

"Take cover, *amigos!*" Bismark quickly leaped behind Dawn, hiding under her tail. Then he peered back out at the brush. "Be gone, you beasts! Beat it, I say! Shoo! Scram!"

But the brush thrashed again. The leaves on the ground trembled with each heavy, approaching step. "Look!" Tobin gasped. The fire in his mouth had cooled somewhat, but it was still difficult for him to speak. "Someone is coming out!"

Dawn narrowed her eyes and bared her claws, preparing to defend herself and her friends. But when the foliage parted at last, the fox let her muscles relax. The animals that emerged were a bush kangaroo; a group of pointy-eared bilbies—small rabbit-like creatures; and a mother bandicoot with her babies—mice-like marsupials with long snouts. Dawn exhaled. Most of these creatures were tiny, timid, and harmless.

But Bismark, his face still half-hidden in the fox's fur, groped wildly on the ground for a stick. He finally managed to wrap his paw around a puny twig. "Stand back, I tell you! *En garde!*" he shouted, blindly waving it to and fro. "I am a powerful predator, a convincing carnivore, a...a ... Well, you don't want to mess with me!"

"Bismark, calm down," Dawn said firmly.

Finally, the sugar glider peeked out at the new arrivals. He guffawed. "Pah! Look at these little nincompoops!" he cried, stepping free of the fox. "What were you two so scared of, hmm? I could take them out with a single flap!"

Tobin cocked his scaly head in concern. The small animals were moving sluggishly. He blinked his beady eyes and looked closer. "Oh goodness," he breathed. "Something's wrong with them!"

Dawn nodded in agreement. These creatures

could do no harm even if they wanted to. The kangaroo was retching and coughing. The bilbies slumped to the ground as soon as they had cleared the bushes. And each animal had the same alarming deformity: their bellies were swollen to twice their normal size.

The fox moved forward, her sharp eyes traveling from one animal to the next. "What happened?" she asked.

The bandicoot, who had been tenderly patting the damp brows of her young ones, took a small hop toward the Brigade. With each movement, she winced in a sharp spasm of pain.

"P-p-p … " she began. But each time she opened her mouth, the words caught in her throat with a dry rasp.

Tobin grimaced as he watched the bandicoot cradle her swollen stomach. Finally, she took a deep breath and tried again.

"It's—it's poison!" she cried at last. "We've been poisoned!"

"*Mon dieu*, what did you say? Take back that horrid word! It cannot be true!" Bismark cried. He looked wildly at Dawn.

Dawn lowered her head so that she could peer into the bandicoot's furrowed face. "What poison? Who poisoned you?" she asked.

"You see...we..." the bandicoot began. She paused to sit down. Then she gripped her gut and rolled over slowly with a low, weak yowl. "Just...a moment.... My... apologies," she stammered.

"Take your time," Tobin said softly. He lowered his snout sympathetically and listened carefully to the bandicoot's faint voice.

"After the big crash two nights ago, we found dozens of fallen pomelos. We had a feast," she explained. "But then..." she glanced at her sick children and shook her head side-to-side. "Well, next thing you know, our mouths are on fire. And then the poison spread and our insides burned, too. We've been sick ever since!"

"Oh goodness!" Tobin cried. He glanced at each of the animals nervously. "This is all from eating pomelos?"

"That's the only thing it could be," said the bandicoot. "We didn't eat anything else." Again, she grimaced with pain and rolled over, exposing the tight, swollen skin stretched across her stomach. "And the pain keeps getting worse."

"*Mon dieu*! Did you two hear what that bunny rabbit just said?" Bismark exclaimed. "The invasion! The poison! The horror! Everything the aye-aye said is true!

Star creatures have come to Earth. They've come to attack us!"

The fox raised an eyebrow at the sugar glider. "Slow down, Bismark. We know only one thing right now: these animals ate something poisonous."

The pangolin swallowed hard and tried his best to look calm. But as his eyes darted anxiously toward the animals' swollen stomachs, he couldn't help but glance down at his own. A faint growl rose through its smooth, gray skin. He hoped the sound meant that he was simply in need of a meal.

Tobin turned to the bandicoot. "Your mouths… it felt like they were on fire, you said?"

The bandicoot and her babies nodded. "And it felt like flames in our throats, too," said the mother.

"And then burning hot pangs in our tummies!" said one of the babies.

"Little creatures—so foolish," began Bismark. "I would never have eaten the fruit! And neither would my *compadres*. Everyone knows you can't trust anything that looks less than *perfecto*. That's why I always trust myself!" The sugar glider smoothed the fur on his scalp and shot a wink at the fox.

"It's never wise to eat something that appears unusual," agreed Dawn. "I'm glad I stopped you," she said to Tobin. "Those pomelos could have been poisoned, too."

Tobin's scales shuddered with dread. Then, while Dawn and Bismark continued to question the bandicoot mother, the pangolin crept over to the babies.

"If you don't mind me asking," he whispered, glancing at his preoccupied friends, "how much did you eat?"

"Well," began one, "we all shared a wedge...."

"... so maybe five bites each?" said another.

"Are you for real, *amigo*?" demanded Bismark, suddenly popping up beside Tobin's snout. "Thinking about your stomach at a time like this? *Mon dieu*, you're truly consumed with consumption...eager about eating ...fiendish about food! These tots could be barfing their brains out, and you'd still be planning a snack."

But Tobin just sighed with relief. Five bites for these baby bandicoots would be equivalent to an entire pomelo for him. And he'd barely taken a taste. Plus, his stomach didn't hurt. He had nothing to worry about, he reasoned.

"Five bites each?" The bush kangaroo hopped forward and joined the group. "You lil' mates must feel awful!" He shook his head in dismay. "I barely ate any, and I got as sick as a snake in a sandstorm!"

Tobin gulped. "Barely any?" he asked.

The kangaroo nodded. "One little bite and I knew something was wrong. My mouth was burning hot. I stopped right after that. And I felt all right… at first. But soon I started to sweat. Then everything ached. And then came the worst." The kangaroo's face crumpled in agony. "My insides started to swell and burn. Like a raging fire, I tell you!"

"But…you seem alright now," insisted Tobin. "You hopped over just fine!"

"Well, *bien sûr*! What'd you expect?" Bismark threw a flap around the kangaroo's back. The glider lifted his chin with pride. "How many times have I told you, *amigos*: we marsupials are the strongest animals in the forest! Invincible, I say! Immune to sickness, disease, even death!" The sugar glider puffed out his chest. "Poison? Pah! More like peanuts, I'd say. 'Tis nothing to the mighty marsupial!"

"I wish you were right, mate," said the kangaroo, "but alas, I doubt even the biggest, strongest animal in the forest could handle this poison. It felt the same way the time I ate poisoned mushrooms. Anyway, one taste of this fruit and my pouch blew up. Three times the size, I'd say. Looked like it might explode…that is, until I ate some blue flowers."

At this, Dawn's ears pricked on end. "You mean the blue flowers with the deep orange centers?" she asked. "The ones with the blue petals and blue leaves?"

"Yes," said the kangaroo. "Those are the ones. They work like magic...though I still don't feel quite like myself—a couple hops and I'm wiped. Unfortunately, I only had a few blossoms. Left over from the time I ate those poisoned mushrooms. Nearly died from those, too."

Nearly died? Tobin's heart began to pound.

"Those petals *do* work like magic," said Dawn. "They can flush almost anything out of your system." She eyed the group of sick animals. "We must find more *now* for everyone to eat."

"That's what we've been trying to do," said the bandicoot mother. "But it's the strangest thing: we haven't been able to find them! We've checked all the usual places, but everywhere we look, the flowers are gone!"

"Maybe other sick animals got there first?" offered Tobin.

"Maybe..." said the bandicoot, "but we've all been sticking together. Plus, there should be more than enough flowers for everyone. They usually grow in huge fields."

Dawn furrowed her brow. First, an unfamiliar poison, then the sudden disappearance of its cure? This seemed like more than a coincidence.

"Will you help us?" asked one of the bilbies, staring up at the fox. He held his stomach then squeezed his eyes tight, as if trying to shut out the pain.

"Of course we'll help," replied Dawn.

"*Bien sûr!*" echoed Bismark.

Tobin nodded as well. But then he paused. Before they set out, should he tell his friends about tasting the pomelo? He glanced down at his stomach. It hadn't grown larger. No, he decided, quickly dismissing the thought. He'd barely tasted the fruit. He had nothing to worry about. Nothing at all.

Chapter Nine
BLUE FLOWERS

"We must find the invaders—the creatures behind all this creepy chaos, this foreign fracas, this poisonous plague!" Bismark yelled, pointing a flap to the north. Then he picked up his twig again and brandished it around like a sword. "It's time to fight them!" he declared. Then he paused. "Whoever they are . . . ."

"Oh goodness," moaned Tobin. His belly was lurching. Was it from fear—or something worse? Panic or poison? He couldn't tell.

"I think we need to find Iris," he said, taking a small step forward. "She was right about the poison. And she said she knows some sort of secret. Maybe she has more information… about the invaders and the fallen star."

"Chitchat with that hideous aye-aye? Or fight for sweet victory against the star creatures?" Bismark tapped his friend on the scalp. "Come on, *amigo*, use that scaly head of yours!"

Dawn, who had been pacing thoughtfully through the trees, came to a sudden stop. "No. We must find the blue flowers," she said. Her voice was quiet but decisive.

"What? *Qué? Quoi?*" Bismark threw up his flaps and protested with a stomp. "What good is a little blue flower against an army of aliens? We must stop them… before they destroy all that is earthly and sweet! No one poisons my fruit and gets away with it!"

Tobin opened his mouth to suggest finding Iris once more. But then the fox lifted her snout, revealing her amber eyes. Their intensity made Tobin stop short.

"Iris was right about the poison," said Dawn, "but we can't assume she was right about everything. No one has actually seen a star creature. And we don't know for certain who poisoned the pomelos." She looked off toward the horizon. "All we know is that the sick animals need our help. And the flowers will cure them. Finding the blue flowers as soon as possible is our priority." The fox shook her head with worry. "We don't know what this poison might do to them if it's left untreated for too long."

The sugar glider flung his twig into the brush. "If you insist, *mon amour.*" He sighed, embracing the fox's leg. "But let the record show that I proposed brawn, bravery, and battle!"

Tobin gulped and cradled his stomach. He wanted to find Iris and get more answers, but his fear of the poison was growing, so he sided with Dawn instead. "Yes," he said, bobbing his snout. "We should find the cure." But then he remembered the words of the ailing animals. "How though? Where? The blue flowers are gone!"

Dawn shook herself free of the glider, who was still gripping her leg. "I know of another flower field," she said, determined. "But it's some distance away, near the springs where the water bubbles up from under the ground. It's the perfect place for these flowers to grow. We must leave at once."

Without another word, Dawn sprang toward the hills, leading the Brigade at a brisk pace. Bismark kept up, soaring just overhead. Tobin, however, fell behind after just a short while.

"Giddyap, my scaly *amigo*! You're cramping our style, slowing our strides, messing our mojo!" Bismark cried from the treetops. "If we're not going to fight, we should at least move with speed!"

"I'm...I'm...coming..." the pangolin gasped, doing his best to sound chipper. But his voice came out strained, and his breathing was heavy and ragged. The pangolin was never the speediest of the group, but this sort of sluggishness felt unfamiliar...different.

Dawn glanced over her shoulder. Not only did Tobin sound fatigued, but his eyes looked a bit dull as well. "Are you okay?" she asked, slowing down.

"Oh goodness, I'm...I'm fine! Here...here I come!" the pangolin panted, plodding up to the fox.

Dawn paused and narrowed her eyes at the pangolin, examining his tired face. But then she turned to the horizon. "Let's go," she commanded, bounding across the plain. "The springs and the flowers are this way." They continued on their journey, but after several twists and turns, their destination was still nowhere in sight.

"Um, Dawn, are we almost there?" Tobin squeaked. "I'm not sure I like the looks of this place."

The pangolin grimaced. But he was less concerned with the barren, dried-up surroundings than with the heat forming in his gut. He wanted to believe it was hunger, but with each step he took, the burning grew more intense until it felt like a fire blazing inside of him. He wasn't sure how much longer he could walk.

"*Si, si,* I second the scaly one," said Bismark, eyeing the unfamiliar land with disgust. "What is this terrible place? There's not a single fruit tree in sight! And I don't see any water, either. Are we lost?"

Tobin felt panic rise in his chest. The burning was growing ever hotter now; it felt as though flames were lapping against his sides. He needed the blue flowers, but how would he ever make it to the field if they didn't even know the way? A sharp pain pierced his belly. He couldn't go any farther. He would have to tell his friends the truth.

"Dawn..." he began.

The fox looked back over her shoulder.

"I have to tell you something." Tobin gulped. "I...I—"

"Wait!" cried the fox, cutting him off. She held up a paw; it was glistening with drops of fresh water. "The springs," she said. "We found them." Then, with confidence in her eyes, Dawn gestured west, where the glint of the moon's reflection shone in a distant pool.

"Oh thank heavens, we made it!" Tobin said. The sight of the water gave him a small spurt of energy, and he pressed ahead of his friends with an awkward gallop, eager to arrive at the shore where the flowers grew. There was no need to confess—he would be all right after all.

But when he got to the edge of the pool, the pangolin quickly skidded to a halt. There wasn't a single flower in sight.

Breathless and confused, Tobin stood still for a moment, allowing his claws to sink into the soft, silty soil. He blinked hard, not trusting his small, beady eyes. But when he opened them once again, he knew his poor sight wasn't the problem. There was nothing growing here. Just some reeds and weeds poking up from the lake bed.

Where were all the flowers?

The pangolin's pointy snout swiveled as he gazed up and down the lake, desperately looking for the blue blossoms.

"What in the name of all gliders?" said Bismark, landing beside the shore. He kicked a small stone into the lake with a *plop* and turned to Dawn. "Where in the world are the flowers?"

"I don't understand," whispered Dawn, pausing beside her Brigade-mates. "This is where they always grow. At this time of year, this place should be blooming with them."

Perplexed, Dawn traced the shoreline, plodding through shallow puddles and nosing through feathered grass. Slowly, her paws weighed down with mud, she rounded a bend and descended a small slope. Then, abruptly, she stopped.

"Tobin, Bismark!" she called.

The pangolin and sugar glider raced up behind her.

"What is it, my lady?" asked Bismark. "Have you found the flowers?"

The fox did not answer. She only stared straight ahead with alarm.

Bismark and Tobin looked at her with concern. Then they followed her gaze and gasped.

Yes, the fox had been right.

On the ground, a single blue petal fluttered in the breeze. The flowers were certainly here. Or, at least, they *had* been.

For there, at the trio's paws, sat a small pile of upturned earth. And next to it was another. And another.

And another, and another, and another: small mounds of dirt with a hole in the center of each.

Just like the mounds near Bismark's tree.

Just like the mounds at the fallen star.

Chapter Ten
STARSPEAK

"*Mon dieu*! Don't you realize what this means?" Bismark cried. "First the fruit, now the flowers! The star creatures have struck again!" The sugar glider kicked at one of the mounds. "I told you we should have gone after them!"

Tobin looked at the bare earth by his paws. It was like a graveyard, with row after row of the chillingly familiar mounds evenly spaced out across the field. The sight made his scent glands twitch and his belly burn with the most extreme heat he'd felt yet. He looked up to his leader, panic in his eyes.

"Oh goodness, Dawn—could it really be? Did the invaders poison the fruit *and* steal the cure?" he asked.

"We still can't be certain," said Dawn, sniffing at one of the holes. "But these mounds were by the poisoned pomelos...and now in the flower field, too. I do think that somehow everything is connected."

Tobin gulped. If there really were invaders and they had stolen the flowers, then how could the Brigade ever retrieve them? They didn't even know where these invaders were...or *who* they were...or what they looked like. "Wh-what are we going to do?" he panted. A wave of nausea shot through him, and he cringed. He needed those flowers.

"I'll tell you what we should do!" said the sugar glider, leaping atop a small rock. "We should do as I said all along: take action! Seize the star creatures! Show them our skills and our strength!" Bismark extended a flap, and nearly toppled over.

Tobin cocked his head. "But—"

"But *nada, amigo*," said Bismark. Let your glider friend handle this. Watch and learn, I say. Watch and learn from your magnificent maestro." Bismark cleared his throat and cupped his tiny hands to his mouth.

"*Kaputo! Faluto*! *Saluto*! Greetings, minions from the moon!" he began, shouting out into the forest. "It is I, Bismark, the official ambassador for your valley vacation! Do not be afraid! Show yourselves! *Eep Ork, Zip Zop Zoop*!"

"Bismark, what in the world are you saying?" Tobin croaked. His voice could barely carry over his heavy breathing. Not only had the heat in his belly increased; his limbs had grown weak and wobbly, and he was struggling to keep up with his friends. "If the star creatures are out there," he panted, "you're going to lead them right to us!"

"*Exactemente, correctomundo*, that's precisely right, *pangolino*!" Bismark replied. "You see, while you may not understand, I, in fact, am fluent in Starspeak. Once the invaders hear their language of the skies, they'll think they've found some friends and come out of hiding. And *that's* when we strike. When we get back at them for poisoning us! When we take control!" Bismark took a bow. "The plan is foolproof!"

He turned toward the trees and shouted again. "Yoo-hoo, moonies! *Beep beep, boop boop*! Don't worry! We shall welcome you in peace!" He shot an exaggerated wink at his friends.

Tobin shook his head. He didn't like the sound of this plan at all.

Dawn walked along the shoreline, ignoring Bismark's rantings and trying to sort through her thoughts. She stared at the mounds and sighed. The priority must be to cure the sick animals, she reasoned. But she didn't know of any more fields where the blue flowers grew. And even if she did, whoever was stealing the flowers seemed to be one step ahead of them.

"*Oi*! Moonie-loonies! Come out, come out, wherever you are!" Bismark's high-pitched call pierced the night.

"Oh goodness, Bismark," said Tobin. "I don't think that sounds much like a star creature language ..." he began, but he stopped short when his keen ears detected a sound—a faint humming in the distance.

Tobin tilted his head. "Do you hear that?" he asked. He took a step closer to Dawn.

Bismark and Dawn craned their necks and listened. Their eyes grew wide.

The sound had grown clearer now. It echoed through the night sky, low and repetitive, like some sort of mysterious chant.

"Holy glider!" yelped Bismark. The sugar glider cowered in fear...but then suddenly stood tall with pride. "My gibberish...I mean...my *fluent* Starspeak... was a success! See? I told you my plan would work!" The sugar glider turned to Dawn and beamed.

But the fox quickly shushed him, raising a paw to her mouth. "Everyone, quiet," she whispered. She angled herself toward the wind and stretched her ears at full length, trying to make out the vague, rhythmic call. It was a strange sound. Nothing they'd ever heard before:

"*I...I...*"

It sounded like an eerie chorus. Dawn listened closely.

"*I...I...*"

The fox focused her gaze and stared out into the darkness, trying to see who was chanting.

"Look! There!" She gasped. At the base of a hill in the distance was a glow...a small ball of light... a light that hadn't been there just moments before, she was certain.

The fox narrowed her eyes and drew in her breath. Then, silently, she directed her friends toward the sight, gesturing with her paw.

"*Mon dieu!*" Bismark cried. "What foul spirit have my nonsense words summoned? I was only speaking gobbledygook, I swear!" The sugar glider wrapped himself in the trembling skin of his flaps.

"Shhh!" Dawn commanded. She centered her gaze on the ghostly glow. How unusual to see a light coming from somewhere other than the sky. Was it some sort of shiny stone? A reflection, perhaps? Another water source nearby?

Slowly, the fox moved forward, hoping to see it more clearly.

But before she could focus on it again, the light moved. It zipped back and forth, then hovered above the grass at the bottom of the hill.

Dawn froze.

This was no stone. This was no pond. The light was coming from something moving.

A chill ran down the fox's spine as she remembered the aye-aye: her talk of invaders...her words of warning: "You shall know when you see the glow. Beware the glow!"

Chapter Eleven
THUNK!

"Oh *mon dieu!*" screeched Bismark. "The glow! The glow! It's a star creature in the flesh! Or rather, a star creature in the...in the...er...whatever it's made of!"

Dawn's eyes widened as she watched the eerie, phantomlike glow dart around the clearing. What was it? Could it really be an invader? The fox dug her claws into the earth. It was time to find out. "Let's go!" she commanded.

"Finally! Just as I've been saying—it's time for battle!" Bismark cried. "*Vamanos, mes amis*—on your mark, get set, charge!"

In a flash, the sugar glider grabbed onto the fox's blue cape, which jolted him forward as Dawn sprinted down the path. Tobin, meanwhile, staggered to his feet, holding his stomach gingerly and taking uneasy steps after his friends.

"*Dios mio*, do you see how it flashes and gleams!?" Bismark cried, his eyes transfixed by the glowing creature's rapid, blinking movements at the bottom of the hill. "It's made of moonlight—the stuff of stars!"

Dawn squinted. Bismark was right: the creature looked like a small orb twinkling with a pale blue light. It was unlike any living being she had ever seen. What would the creatures look like up close? What did they want? Could the Brigade defeat them? She pressed forward, uneasy, but eager to get some answers all the same.

Tobin huffed and puffed after her, but he was starting to wobble with every step, and he suddenly felt strangely heavy. He paused to catch his breath. "Oh goodness!" he gasped, looking down. His belly had started to swell!

Tobin gulped. He needed a flower more than ever now—and if the star creatures were snatching them, this could be their best chance of finding one.

"Keep…going…." Despite his pain, Tobin urged himself on, taking deep, steadying breaths. They were nearly there now. The orb was just a few paw's lengths ahead. But as they drew closer to it, they could see something more. In the circle of blue light was a vague sort of outline. The star creature was made of more than just light!

The three friends squinted, struggling to make out the form. But then—

Poof!

The moon slipped behind the clouds, and just like that, the glow vanished.

The trio skidded to a halt.

"*Quoi!* What diabolical demon is this?" uttered Bismark, bewildered. "Where'd the little star-critter go?"

Dawn lunged at the spot where the glow had been just a moment ago and dug furiously at the ground. "It has to be here," she shouted, churning her paws, but then she recoiled as her claws scratched hard stone. The ground underneath was solid rock. The glower was nowhere to be found.

Tobin clutched his stomach and couldn't help

79

but let out a moan of despair. His vision was fuzzy and his sweaty brow throbbed. Everything seemed hopeless. No glow, no flower, no cure.

But then the moon peeked through the clouds, and the pangolin glimpsed something blue in the distance. He blinked.

"Oh my, look! Look, both of you!" he cried. "There it is!"

Dawn and Bismark followed his gaze.

"Wait, no." The pangolin grew confused. He realized what he saw wasn't glowing, exactly.

He squinted again. Then he turned to the fox. To his surprise, her face was stretched into a wide smile.

"Dawn? Wh-what is it?" he asked.

The fox eagerly bounded up the hill's slope. "Tobin, it's a flower!" she yelled over her shoulder. "It's a blue flower! The star creature led us right to it!"

As the Brigade crested the hill and the moon rose above the clouds, the land before them finally came into view. And that's when they saw it: a whole field of blossoms swaying against the sky, their orange centers and broad blue leaves flickering in the night like small flames. The trio couldn't help but take a moment to pause and admire the sight.

"Aha! I know what you two are thinking: my plan was pure genius!" Bismark exclaimed, thrusting a fist toward the sky. "I successfully summon a star creature …and then it leads us straight to the flowers! That's what I call a win-win, *amigos*! A marsupial miracle! A Bismarkian boom!"

"Thank goodness! Thank goodness! The sick animals are going to be all right!" Tobin said with a gulp.

"Yes," said Dawn, "let's gather the flowers quickly!"

At once, the fox and the sugar glider bounded across the slope toward the field. But when Tobin tried to follow, he felt suddenly stuck to the ground. "Oomph!" He grunted as he attempted another step. But it was no use. He looked down at his stomach in horror. The skin was pale and taut, and it brushed the ground when he walked. His stomach was so swollen now, he couldn't even wrap his arms around it!

"Oh no," he said, struggling to lift his foot. At last, he managed to take a step forward, but the movement sent a sharp jolt through his scales. "W-wait…I…I can't…"

"What are you doing, *muchacho*?" Bismark flapped back toward his friend and eyed him holding his belly. "Your stomach, *amigo*? Really? Truly? Now? This is no time to be hungry! We've got to get to the fields!"

"I … I know…" Tobin sputtered. "I just—"

"You just *quoi*?" Bismark asked. "What's the problemo? The issue? The hold up?"

Dawn looked back over her shoulder. "Tobin," she said sharply. "Come on. The sick animals need the flowers. You said so yourself. We must hurry."

Tobin swallowed hard and attempted another step, but his body seized in agony. "I know…but I…" He took a deep breath. He couldn't hide it from his friends any longer. "I do, too!" Tobin cried at last. "I need the flowers, too!"

Bismark's mouth fell open. Dawn took a step back toward her friend.

"Oh no…" she whispered, catching sight of his swollen belly. "You ate the fruit!?"

Tobin desperately nodded his head. "Yes!" he cried, confessing at last. ""I did. I tasted the poisoned pomelo!"

"*Mon dieu*!" Bismark cried. "*Quelle horreur!* How do you feel, *pangolino*? Are you all right?" But before Tobin could answer, the sugar glider's mood quickly changed from concerned to annoyed. He puffed out his chest and raised his flaps in the air. "I can't believe you kept this from us!" he exclaimed. "Don't you know that the Brigade shares all? Tell him, *mi amore*," he said, looking up at the fox. "Don't I always say everything on my mind? Don't I always pour my heart out to you, like a beautiful song?"

"I-I didn't want you to be worried," said Tobin, looking pleadingly at his leader. Then he tried to smile. "Besides, it's all going to be okay now, anyway, isn't it?"

The pangolin pointed his snout toward the sea of flowers swaying in the field below. Even under the thick blanket of clouds overhead, the flowers seemed to radiate a bright blue. "I'll be fine in no time," he said. "All the animals will be. Everything is going to be—"

Thunk.

Tobin stopped mid-sentence. One of the blossoms had just jerked down and out of sight.

Another one disappeared, just as quickly as the first!

Thunk.

And another one, gone, before the Brigade's very eyes.

Thunk! Thunk! Thunk!

Faster and faster now, the flowers disappeared

underground. Tobin clutched his stomach. Maybe he wouldn't be fine after all.

Thunk! Thunk! Thunk!

Gone.

Gone.

Gone.

Chapter Twelve
"I... I..."

"Mon dieu! It's the invaders!" yelled Bismark.

It was all happening so fast. The blue blossoms were disappearing into the ground, one after another, without a trace.

Thunk! Thunk! Thunk!
Thunk! Thunk! Thunk!

The fox raced down the hill, with Bismark clinging to her snakeskin cape and Tobin trundling behind.

Dawn sprinted now, desperate to reach the flowers. Desperate to save as many as she could. With one final leap, she was there. But each time she grabbed for a flower, her claws only grasped empty air. The flowers were being sucked into the earth faster than she could react.

"You're moving too slowly, my love! Try like this!" Bismarck shouted as he scurried toward a flower, flaps outstretched.

Thunk!

The blossom jerked underground so quickly, it spun the glider around like a miniature cyclone.

"*Mon dieu*! A little help here, amigo!" the glider cried out to Tobin as he staggered dizzily about.

"I'm coming!" called Tobin. "Oof!" The pangolin stretched out a claw, struggling to reach one of the flowers.

Thunk!

It disappeared before he could grab it. "Oomph!" He stumbled after another.

Thunk!

"No!"

Thunk! Thunk! Thunk!

"No! No! No!"

The pangolin's efforts were to no avail. The

moon had slipped behind a cloud, making it difficult to see, and with the added weight and pain of his boiling belly, he was far too slow to stop the flowers from going under.

"By the stars—it's a riot, a rampage, a raid!" Bismark cried.

Dawn looked around helplessly. Before her eyes, the entire field was becoming entirely barren of blue— each and every flower was disappearing into the depths of the earth.

Finally, defeated and out of breath, the Brigade found themselves standing in the middle of a blossomless field.

"*Oh mon dieu*. Sick animals...no flowers...no cure. *Pas du tout*! We are doomed! Destroyed! Done for, I tell you!" shrieked Bismark. "Well, at least you are, *amigo*," he added, glancing sideways at Tobin.

Dawn shot a searing stare at the sugar glider.

"Oh goodness," said Tobin. His voice trembled as his stomach lurched in pain. "How could this get any worse?"

"*I...I...*"

The trio froze—the eerie voices were back! Dawn's ears stood high and taut. She raised a paw to her mouth to hush her friends.

"*I...I...*" The strange call came again.

Bismark's eyes nearly bulged out of his tiny skull. "*Mon dieu*! Does that answer your question, my scaly chum? This is how things get worse!" He gulped. "It's the star creatures! First they're after the flowers.... And now they're after us!" The sugar glider quickly leaped behind Dawn's tawny rear leg and covered his face with his flaps.

Nervously, Tobin looked into the distance. His throat tightened and his stomach churned as he awaited the eerie blue glow. But when the creatures came into view, Tobin cocked his head in confusion. "Wait...." He took a tiny step forward and focused his beady eyes. These creatures weren't glowing at all! In fact, they appeared to be covered in something familiar: soft, light brown fur.

Bismark gasped. "*Mon dieu*! The invaders are even wilier than I thought!" He pointed with one flap. "They've performed some sort of dark magic to disguise themselves! To transform into earthly animals! To make themselves like...mice...or rabbits...or..."

"...lemurs," Dawn finished.

"Yes, precisely, that's it!" exclaimed Bismark. "They've disguised themselves as little lemurs!"

The fox shook her head. "No, Bismark," she

said. "They *are* lemurs."

"*Quoi?*" Bismark examined the chanting creatures once more. Dawn was right—they were just lemurs: small, furry, and—dare he admit it?—cute.

"What a letdown," he grumbled, kicking the hard, dry ground at his feet then wincing at the throbbing in his toe.

"But why are they here?" asked Tobin. His body trembled with pain, forcing him to sit. "Do they have something to do with this?"

"It certainly is odd," said Dawn. She eyed the dozens of chanting animals with suspicion. Although they were not the star creatures, there was something quite strange about them. Their eyes were glazed over, and they were moving slowly and stiffly, as though they were in some sort of trance. "Let's watch them," said the fox, scanning the terrain. She gestured toward a large rock near the edge of the flower field. "We'll hide over there."

Quickly, the fox bounded behind the stone. The sugar glider followed, but Tobin struggled to stand. "I don't think I can go that far." His voice came out in a whisper.

With some gentle pushing and pulling, Dawn and Bismark helped the pangolin move out of sight.

"Look at those weird little fuzz balls," Bismark grunted, peering beyond the rock's edge. "What are they trying to say? 'I, I,' *what*?"

The sugar glider watched as the furry animals came to a stop in the barren field, just a few tree-lengths away. Then he saw them pull something from the folds of their fur.

Bismark squinted at the lemurs, curious. What were they holding? At last, the moon reappeared from behind a curtain of clouds, allowing the sugar glider to see more clearly. The lemurs were holding sprigs of tiny red berries…and then they were swallowing them whole: stems, flesh, pits, and all.

"Really? Truly? *Vraiment*? This is the time for a snack?" Bismark wondered. "What lazy, hunger-brained *hombres*! I *knew* they couldn't be the star creatures!" He gave a small laugh. "Pah! Star creatures dressed as little lemurs? Who would have ever imagined such an *absurdo* idea…?"

But then his voice trailed off. Something very strange was happening. In a matter of moments, the animals had undergone a total transformation. They were no longer the slow, snacking creatures they were a moment ago. They were crazed blurs, zipping and zooming across the field with unnatural quickness and speed.

"Oh goodness! What's going on?" the pangolin exclaimed.

"I don't know," said the fox. "But this is very unusual. We don't know what these lemurs will do next or what is causing this strange behavior. So stay hidden."

Tobin obliged at once, crouching down to the ground and cradling his swollen belly. Bismark, however, stood on tiptoe, his big, bulbous eyes growing wide.

He stared in awe as another group of lemurs popped the fruit in their mouths. Then, just like the others, they started to zip and zoom across the field like lightning bugs.

Bismark's gaze narrowed, his expression shifting from awe to envy.

"If I could just get one of those little fruits..." he mused, tapping his fingers together. "I mean, *mon dieu*! Look what they did for those slow, lazy lemurs! Imagine what they'd do for a sugar glider!"

Completely captivated, Bismark crept past the rock's jagged edge and carefully made his way toward the frenzied lemurs. "After all, I am naturally swift and slick," he continued to himself. "With these little berries,

I'd be undefeatable, unbeatable, invincible!"

"Bismark!" Dawn's voice rang out from behind the rock.

"All is well, *mon amour!*" he yelled, not even bothering to look back. "I shall join you again in *uno momento....*" Bismark marched on, nearing the buzzing lemurs. "We may not have gotten the flowers, but I'm going to get something even better!" he reasoned. "*Si, si.* My beloved Dawn won't be able to resist me once I get my paws on that fruit."

"BISMARK!" both Dawn and Tobin called out this time.

The sugar glider gave an exasperated sigh and glanced over his shoulder. "*Que paso?*" he asked. "What is it?"

"Come back here! Now!" the fox commanded.

"Huh?" Bismark said. Then he scanned his surroundings, finally registering the scene before him. The lemurs weren't just zipping and zooming at random. They were forming a ring...around him!

"*Oh mon dieu!* Never mind—keep your berries! They're all yours!" he yelled, backing away. "Keep them all! I don't need them anyway...I am *magnifique* enough as it is!"

But the lemurs weren't listening. Or, if they

were, they ignored him. They moved in closer and closer, their bodies vibrating so fast now, they appeared as a single furry blur. Bismark's breaths turned from shallow to heaving as the dozens of creatures pressed in on him. Chanting and chanting. Louder and louder.

"Eeeeeeeek!" The sugar glider released a bloodcurdling scream as the hoard of lemurs closed in, their eager paws reaching for him. "Dawn! Tobin!" he cried, cowering under his flaps. "HELP!"

Chapter Thirteen
PANGOLIN POOF

"This is it! This is the end! I shall meet my death at the paws of these loco lemurs!" Bismark cried. The circle of crazed animals tightened around him, grabbing him and pushing him along. "Get your paws off me, you brutes! Stick to your fancy fruits and stay away from *moi*!"

Dawn leaped out of the rock's shadow as the lemurs tried to shove Bismark across the field. "We have to help him," she said, beckoning Tobin to follow.

"Ouch!" The pangolin took a step but yelped in pain. His stomach churned and felt like it was on fire. He curled up in a crescent and clutched his belly, but the flames he felt inside did not lessen.

Dawn spun around. She drew in a sharp breath as she caught sight of her friend writhing and reeling on the ground. "Take a deep breath," she said, moving back to the pangolin's side. But she couldn't help glancing anxiously over at Bismark. She could barely see his gray pelt through the mass of surrounding lemurs. "Will you be okay?" she asked Tobin.

The pangolin let out a grunt and gave a small nod.

Dawn placed a paw on Tobin's trembling scales. "I'll be right back," she promised. "Just hold on." Then she sprang out to rescue the sugar glider from the circle of lemurs.

"Oh goodness!"

Dawn heard Tobin cry out behind her, but she couldn't stop.

"OH NO!"

Tobin cried out again. Dawn's heart pounded in her chest.

"NOOOOOO!"

At last, Dawn came to a halt. She had no choice —

this cry was different. Desperate. What was happening to her friend? The fox glanced back worriedly—then she gasped.

"I'm…" Tobin's eyes bulged from his face. "I'm gonna…"

Dawn's throat felt tight at the sight. Tobin was no longer curled in a ball—he was splayed on the ground, spine arched, tail lifted high in the air.

"I'm gonna…BLOOOOOOOW!" Tobin yelped. His entire body shook. "Ohhh...Myyyyyy…Goooodness!!!!"

With a giant *whoosh*, Tobin's scent glands unleashed behind him. His body jolted forward as his defensive spray shot out of him in a dense, greenish cloud, a truly terrible stench.

Dawn shielded her snout with her tail, but even through her thick fur, she could smell the pangolin's spray. Although Tobin's poofs were never pleasant, the poisonous pomelo rendered this one absolutely ghastly. Dawn crouched low to the ground, further away from the horrific cloud overhead. But even still, she coughed. It was the most foul, awful scent she had ever smelled in her life—so bad, in fact, that it stung her nostrils, her eyes, and her throat.

"By all that is heavenly!" Bismark cried, still

struggling under his captors. "I am certainly doomed now! If not at the hands of these crazed fur balls, then from the fumes of my foul friend!"

Bismark pawed desperately at the lemurs' claws. "In the name of all that is sweet, release me! I need my flaps to wave away this repulsive odor! And you, *mes amis*, should do the same!"

But even through pained coughs and watery eyes, the lemurs held fast to Bismark and continued their chant.

"*I…*"—*gasp*—"*I…*"—*cough.* "*I…I…*"—*wheeze*—*gasp*—*cough.*

Under the harsh, green cloud, the sugar glider coughed and sputtered. "Good-bye, my sweet fox! Fare-thee-well, my fair maiden! How I wish my dying breaths could have been filled with your sweet smell instead of the scaly one's stench!"

A strong breeze blew, propelling the cloud of poisonous stink across the field and settling directly over the lemurs' heads. All at once, they began to choke. And then they were left with no choice: they were forced to release the sugar glider to grab at their throats, wipe their eyes, and plug their noses.

"*Mon dieu!*" Free to move at last, Bismark wrapped himself in his flaps to protect himself from the deadly fumes. But he was unable to see, and he stumbled forward, back, and in circles until, finally, he collapsed onto his rear. Dizzy and disoriented, he stayed there, huddled in a tiny ball, eyes closed, waiting for the lethal fog to pass.

"Bismark." Sometime later, he heard a voice overhead. "It's okay now. The air has cleared."

It was Dawn. Slowly, Bismark unfurled his flaps and opened a single eye. He sighed with relief. His two friends stood beside him, and he was all right. But where were the lemurs?

The sugar glider opened his other eye and frantically gazed about. Then he gasped.

The lemurs were still there—each and every one of them. But they were no longer zipping or zooming—in fact, they weren't moving at all. No—they were lying flat on the earth: unmoving, unthreatening, and entirely unconscious!

"The poison made Tobin's scent extra powerful," said Dawn, letting out a small, raspy cough. Her amber eyes were teary and bloodshot from the toxic fumes. But as she squinted to survey the passed-out animals, she could not help but betray a small smile. "The lemurs just couldn't take it."

Tobin lowered his snout. "I'm sorry," he said.

"You're sorry?" cried Bismark. "Are you kidding, *muchacho*?" Holding his nose, the sugar glider rose to his feet. "You should be proud, scale-butt! Your special aroma is a knockout!"

"Oh goodness," Tobin said sheepishly. "I suppose the poison was at least good for something!" He let out a tiny giggle. "And I feel a bit better, too. I might not even need the blue flower any—" But Tobin stopped short and winced. The heat had suddenly returned to his belly. The toxic explosion had only provided temporary relief.

Dawn's face creased with concern. But then her eyes darted sideways, and her worry shifted to anger: one of the lemurs had awakened and was staggering to its feet with a groan.

The fox took a firm step toward it. "Who sent you here? Why are you after us?" she demanded. The fox placed a paw on its shoulder and shook it. "Can you hear me?" She looked around at the surrounding field, her amber eyes flickering across the barren ground. "Where are the flowers? Who is taking them?"

The lemur spoke in a weak voice. "I…I…"

"Yes! Yes! Enough with all this 'you, you' talk!" Bismark cried. He waved away one last whiff of the pangolin's spray and sidled up next to the fox. "You, you what?" he demanded, glaring at the lemur. "Out with it!"

"I..." the lemur began. "I...can't remember," he said at last. He shook his head and blinked rapidly. Dawn noticed that the clarity in his eyes was returning. "After all that back and forth, my mind went completely blank."

"Back and forth?" Dawn repeated. "Back and forth between what?" The fox clenched her jaw. This animal wasn't making any sense. She tried once more. "Tell us who sent you here to attack us. Tell us who is taking the flowers!"

But the lemur appeared to be dizzy. His eyes looked bleary and glazed again. "Back and forth..." he repeated. His pupils were moving now, traveling slowly from left to right, left to right, across their sockets. "Back and forth."

The Brigade stared. The lemur tottered on its hind legs. Then he lifted a finger and dangled it in front of his face.

"*I...I...*" he sang, his voice monotone and trance-like once more.

"You, you, *nada*! This is infuriating! The only 'I' here that deserves that much attention is I, I. Me, me. Bismark, Bismark!"

But the lemur continued his chant, as if the glider hadn't spoken. "*I... I...*"

"*Mon dieu,* you can stop now—we heard you! At the very least, you could lower that finger of yours. It's very strange, *muy* creepy. Just like that loony, Iris." The sugar glider grimaced. Then he mussed his hair into a crazed poof on his head, lifted a finger, and screeched. "Remind you of anyone?"

"Bismark, that's it!" cried the fox, her eyes transfixed on his paw.

"A marvelous impression, I know," Bismark boasted. "Just one of my many talents."

"No," Dawn said. Her gaze brightened. "They haven't been saying 'I...I...' They've been saying 'aye-aye'!"

"Aye-Aye Iris!" gasped Tobin, his beady eyes widening.

At the mention of Iris's name, the blurry-eyed lemur let out a shrill yelp then collapsed to the ground. For a brief moment, his pupils grew so wide they looked as if they might burst. Then his eyes snapped shut, and he fainted once more.

"*Mon dieu!*" exclaimed Bismark. "Why are they bringing that creepy *muchacha* into this?" The sugar glider raised a flap to his forehead.

102

"Oh goodness, maybe Iris sent the lemurs to find us," Tobin suggested.

"Yes," agreed Dawn. "It seems like she might have." With narrowed eyes, the fox surveyed her surroundings once more. No flowers. No glower. No leads. She grunted. They needed to find the flowers but, at this point, perhaps the aye-aye was their best bet. "Let's go find her," said Dawn.

With that, the fox set off into the night. Tobin, stomach churning again, followed slowly behind her. And Bismark glided behind the two...but not before he snagged one of the tiny red berries from the lemur's limp, outstretched paw.

Chapter Fourteen
PAT, PAT, PAT

"This mission is loco, I tell you! That aye-aye could be anywhere. We're never going to find her!" The sugar glider stomped his feet then promptly flung the mud off his toes. The Brigade-mates were traveling back through the marshlands just south of the springs, and the ground had turned soggy and soft. "Not that I mind, if you want to know the glider's truth," Bismark continued. "I must say, that Iris is the nastiest, stinkiest-smelling *amiga* I have ever met. She startles the eyes!

She offends the nose!"

"The nose…" mused Tobin. "Yes."

"Thank you, *mon ami*. I was born to provide these kinds of valuable insights," Bismark said. He turned to Dawn. "Hear that, my love? I speak the truth! Even our own malodorous *muchacho* agrees with me."

"No, Bismark," said the pangolin. "I meant I could use my nose to track Iris!"

Tobin eagerly began sampling the odors of the earth with his long, keen snout. "I remember her particular scent well," he said, poking through curtains of reeds. "Kind of tangy…. A little damp…. Somewhat stale…."

Bismark grimaced, but Dawn gave an encouraging nod.

"Let's sniff, let's sniff," muttered Tobin. The pangolin picked up his pace, sending mud splashing behind him, but he quickly drew to a halt.

"Did you find something?" asked Dawn.

"Already, *compadre*?" asked Bismark. "Perhaps I underestimated your schnoz!"

"Oh goodness, no," said the pangolin. "I'm sorry…I…" Tobin swallowed hard, trying to block out the terrible, burning pain that had forced him to stop.

Dawn eyed the pangolin, cradling his belly, then

padded toward him. "You'll be okay," she whispered. The fox placed her paw on Tobin's scales and gave him a tender pat. "Just concentrate. You can lead us to Iris. And that's our best chance at getting you a blue flower."

Encouraged by Dawn's words, Tobin squeezed his eyes shut to focus on his keen sense of smell instead of the burn in his belly. Then, with a determined breath, he proceeded through the brush, extending his snout this way and that.

Dawn and Bismark followed behind him until, after several twists and turns, he paused and snapped his eyes open.

"Oh goodness!" he cried. "I think I've got something!"

Shuffling his legs toward a bed of moss, the pangolin furrowed his brow in concentration. He was inhaling the air faster, deeper, and louder, and his nostrils started to tingle and twitch. "Ooh! I...I think I...I think I...ah...ah...ah-choo!"

Tobin's body rolled backward with the force of a mighty sneeze. Then, opening his eyes, he tried to spot what had tickled his nose.

"Hey! Watch where you're going with that thing!" squeaked a thin, high-pitched voice.

Alarmed, Tobin squinted and turned his head in

all directions. "Who's … who's there?" he asked.

"Down here!"

Tobin looked down at his claws. "Oh my!" he said with a jump. The pangolin had indeed tracked down a creature with his impressive nose. But it was not Aye-Aye Iris. It was a woylie: a tiny, furry, mouse-like marsupial, poking its head up from the moss.

"And be quiet!"

Another popped out from the grass nearby.

"You sniff like a hog!"

"You're ruining our search!"

Two more woylies emerged from the shadows. Together, the four little creatures began to rapidly shout at the pangolin:

"Much too much noise!"

"You're muffling the sound!"

"We need the vibrations!"

"Shhh!"

The pangolin paused. Dawn and Bismark stood at either shoulder, and he looked to them in confusion. "Vibrations?" he asked aloud.

The mice began to titter and squeak.

"Vibrations in the ground!"

"It's how we navigate!"

"Our ears are our eyes!"

"Seismic communication!"

"Yes," Dawn started to explain. "These woylies sense movement in the earth by picking up on vibrations. But usually it is to *avoid* other creatures, not to *search* for them."

"That's right! We know all the footsteps of all the animals in the forest, just like our own paws," piped up the woylie near Tobin's claws. "But tonight we've felt vibrations unlike anything we've ever experienced!"

At this, Dawn's ears perked up. She gathered the four little creatures together in a huddle. "Can you tell us more about them?" she asked.

"Strange movements."

"New sounds."

"Scary ones!"

"We think it's from the thing that got good old Dewey."

A long, whinnying sound rose from the four mice. They had suddenly burst into tears.

"What happened?" asked Tobin.

"Our friend, Dewey, the boar!" sniffled the woylies. "He's…he's...dead!"

The miniature marsupials lowered their eyes to the ground in sorrow. Then they looked back up.

"We're trying to find who's responsible."

"The one who poisoned his pomelo."

"That's who must be making these sounds."

"We must avenge Dewey's death!"

"Pomelo!?" yelped Bismark.

"Poison?" asked Dawn.

"Death?" croaked the pangolin.

The Brigade exchanged terrified glances. The woylies seemed to be putting so much together at once: strange sounds, unusual activity, poisoned fruit. But the poisoned animals the three friends had met weren't dying...yet.

"The poisoned animals we've met have only been sick," said the fox. She paused. "Are you sure it was the pomelo that caused your friend's death?"

The woylies looked toward the ground and nodded. "We're sure," they whispered.

Tobin opened his mouth to speak, but all he could do was tremble and hold his burning belly. His voice and words were failing him. At last, he swallowed hard and closed his dry lips. Perhaps there was nothing to say.

Gently, Dawn placed a paw on Tobin's back. Bismark placed a soothing flap there, too.

"If only he'd had a blue flower," said a woylie. "We met other sick animals, and they told us the blue flowers were the cure."

"Just one and he'd still be here."

"We couldn't find any."

"But we're going to find the culprit!"

Then the four woylies scurried about the moss, pressing their ears to the ground, listening for the vibrations once more.

Dawn gave Tobin a comforting pat and watched the animals at work. Her mind was working through what she had just heard. Perhaps they should follow the lead of the woylies. At least they were on the trail of *something.*

The fox bent low to the ground, straining to pick up on the vibrations, too. Even with her keen sense of hearing and touch, she didn't sense anything unusual coming from the ground.

"Too quiet for you to hear," said a woylie, looking up.

"Here, we'll show you!"

Scurrying before the Brigade, the woylies used their small claws and front teeth to burrow tiny holes in the earth. Then they stuck their whole heads underground. As they listened to the earth's deep whispers, they began to pat their feet to the beat of the silent sensations they felt.

Pat pat pat.

Pat pat pat.

The woylies popped their heads back above ground. "Hear that? That's what we've been feeling all night. And it's getting louder and louder in this part of the forest. We think we're getting closer."

Pat pat pat.

Pat pat pat.

The woylies repeated the sound, patting their paws on the ground.

Bismark shuddered. "Enough of this pestering pat pat patting! That horrible sound reminds me of that hideous aye-aye's fingernail. *Pat pat pat...tap tap tap.* All this creepy noise makes my flaps furl."

Dawn's amber hair stood up along her neck. "Iris." She let out a long breath.

The woylies' eyes widened. "Iris? Who is Iris? Is she the one who poisoned Dewey?"

"We can't say that," said the fox, "but she seems to know more about the poison than anyone else."

"We've been looking for her," added Tobin. "We're hoping to get more information. You see, well ...." He paused and lowered his snout. "I ate the poison, too."

The woylies gasped.

"You must find a flower!"

"Or you'll end up like Dewey!"

Tobin felt a sharp pang in his side. Desperately, he clutched his stomach.

The fox bent her snout toward the woylies and met their wide eyes with her own. "Listen again. Do you hear the sound? Can you lead us to it?"

"Yes!"

"Of course!"

"Anything in honor of Dewey."

"Anything for those who need help!"

At once, the four little creatures pressed their ears back to the ground. Within moments, their faces grew bright. They had picked up the sound once again.

"We've got it!" they cried. "Let's go!"

And with that, the woylies raced off, the Brigade following close behind.

Chapter Fifteen
THE STARLIT CAGE

"Over here!"

"It's getting louder!"

"Hurry up!"

"We're almost there!"

The woylies scurried through the forest, stopping quickly and often to press their tiny ears against the ground, tracking the signals, then moving onward once more.

"Oh goodness, where are they taking us?" asked

Tobin, trundling behind the group.

With a sudden swerve, the woylies led the Brigade into a thicket of tall grass. They ran this way and that, changing direction without warning or, it seemed, sense.

"*Mon dieu*, this is *absolument* absurd!" cried the sugar glider. "All this *pat pat patting* that no one but these nincompoops can hear? *Ridiculo*, I tell you!"

Dawn shot the glider a glare over her shoulder.

But Bismark continued his protests. "You must admit, my dearest, we've gotten nowhere! Gathered *nada*!" The sugar glider flapped faster, just behind the white of Dawn's tail. "Either Iris duped us all with some sort of tricky trap, or these woylies are sending us on a wild goose chase. Or, shall I say, a wild aye-aye chase." Bismark smirked.

But then, the woylies came to an abrupt halt atop a small, rocky hill. Dawn stopped short behind them, causing Bismark to crash against her tawny rear end before collapsing back onto the ground.

"The signal's stopped!"

"We've lost the trail!"

"The sound is gone!"

"It was coming from here!"

The woylies frantically pointed through wiry,

brown grass, down the hill's opposite slope.

The Brigade tiptoed forward and peered past the rocky edge. Below them, nestled in thick blankets of shadow, was the dark looming mouth of a cave.

"Oh goodness," gasped Tobin. The pangolin glanced nervously at the cave's jagged outline and at the pitch-black hue of its depths. "I don't see anything."

"*Si*, where is that atrocious aye-aye? Where's all the *tap tap tapping*?" Bismark asked. "Should we call for her? Shall I shake my tail to attract her attention, perhaps?" The sugar glider peered at the black stripe adorning his backside and gave a self-satisfied nod.

"Hush, Bismark," Dawn scolded. She turned to the woylies. Their eyes were glazed and they swayed on their tiny feet. They were clearly exhausted from their long night of searching. "Can you hear anything else?" she asked them.

The little creatures pressed their ears to the ground once again, but in vain. The *pat pat patting* had ceased, and the night had turned eerily quiet.

"Thank you, all of you," said the fox, bending her snout toward the group. One of the woylies yawned, then, one by one, the others did as well. "Go get some rest," Dawn continued. "We can take it from here."

The woylies nodded and looked gratefully at the

fox. Then they retreated into the darkness, leaving the Brigade alone.

"Keep close, you two," whispered Dawn. "If we stay hidden, we can try to see into the mouth of the cave without being detected."

"Without being detected by *quoi? Qui? Quién?*" The sugar glider stood on his tiptoes and looked skeptically at the cave. "There's *nada* in there. Those wimpy woylies led us astray!"

"Shhh!" Dawn yanked Bismark down by the tail. "Look!" The fox parted the brush with her front paws. Tobin and Bismark both gasped.

The cave's shadows were shifting. And, with the help of the full, luminous moon, the Brigade could make out a strange silhouette emerging from the mouth of the cave. It had frazzled hair, pointed ears, and two extra-long fingers protruding from its wild paws. Tobin squealed and Bismark retched. It was Iris!

"Oh my, thank goodness she's here!" said Tobin excitedly. "We can finally ask her for help!" The pangolin straightened up and made a move toward the cave, but before he could step out of the brush, Dawn pulled him back down to his seat.

"Tobin, wait!" she said. She held a paw to her mouth, keeping her eyes locked on the aye-aye.

Iris was up to something peculiar. She was squatting down on the ground and pressing one ear to the earth, just like the woylies had. Then, with her eyes squeezed shut, she began to slowly tap the earth with one of her extra-long fingers.

Tap tap tap.

Tap tap tap.

"Oh *mon dieu*, it was the aye-aye making those horrific sounds after all!" Bismark cried. He stared at her long, gangly finger and shuddered. "*Blech*! My poor, innocent eyes cannot stand such a hideous sight! She could skewer a squirrel with that thing!"

"But what is she doing with it now?" whispered Tobin.

Iris closed her eyes. Her taps were growing faster, more persistent.

Tap tap tap!

Tap tap tap!

Suddenly, Iris's eyes shot back open. Their bloodshot, orange glare shone in the darkness, and a wave of energy seemed to course through her frame. Then she stood up, threw her head backward, and shrieked. "Rise! Rise, my moonlight beauties! Rise!"

The aye-aye lifted her claws toward the sky. The earth beneath her hind paws began to stir as it grew

119

dotted with tiny mounds. Tiny mounds with holes in the centers. Just like at the fallen star. And Bismark's pomelo tree. And the flower field. Then, suddenly, as if Iris had cast some wicked spell, the earth around Iris became illuminated. Beams of pale, blue light were shooting up from the holes!

"*Dios mio*, what evilness is this?" Bismark gasped. "It's the glow we saw at the flower field. Iris has summoned the star creatures from underground! She's working with the invaders!"

The beams around Iris were brightening. For a moment, the aye-aye appeared to be enclosed in a luminous, starlit cage as dozens and dozens of glowing balls of light came streaming from the mounds around the cave.

Tobin stared at the glowing creatures and the faint shapes he could see through their blue light. Were those tails? Antennae? Claws? Were those pointy things long rows of legs? Or were they layers of fangs? And what were those bulbous bumps? Did the star creatures have multiple heads?

The pangolin gulped and squinted again at the aliens, hoping to see more. But the invaders were too far away and their glow was too bright. He could see nothing for certain, except for the aye-aye, waving one long finger, beckoning the invaders closer. Immediately, they obliged, gathering before her like a constellation of blue stars.

"Good....Yes....Gooooood," Iris hissed. "You've done well, my beauties. Aye-Aye Iris has nearly all the flowers now!"

"*Quoi!? She's* the one with the flowers!?" Bismark sputtered.

"Oh my, she said she would protect us from the star creatures...but she's working with them!" cried Tobin. "She doesn't have a helpful secret—she has an evil one!"

Dawn let out a low, angry growl.

"And now, the final phase of the plan!" Iris cackled. "Aye-Aye Iris must have all the flowers. Then everyone will depend on her! Then everyone will need her! So go! Bring them to her! Harvest them! Cull the last blue flower field at the western plateau!" The aye-aye threw her ragged head back, her stringy fur whipping behind her, and howled.

As Iris let out her horrible shriek, the glowing creatures scrambled over the cave's stony exterior and into the forest depths. In their wake, they left a trail of millions of tiny footprints, as if together they were a single, luminescent centipede slithering through the undergrowth.

"Oh goodness, the glowers are going to get the flowers…again!" wailed the pangolin. He cradled his stomach, wincing at the hot, searing pain. "Why are they doing this?" he sputtered. "Why are the invaders listening to Iris and stealing all of the flowers? What do they want?"

Dawn shook her head, unable to answer.

"Go! Go, my beauties!" Iris cooed. The aye-aye watched with satisfaction as the last of the glowing creatures disappeared over the rocky ground. Then she turned and started to slink back into the cave, her bushy, knotted tail swishing behind her in the freshly churned dirt.

"*Mon dieu*, this is our chance!" Bismark cried. "That aye-aye's a terror, a trickster, a traitor! Let's go get her while the glowers are gone and the going's good!"

The fox stared hard after the vanishing aye-aye, but then she shook her head. "We need to save the flowers," she said. Her tone was firm. "We must cure Tobin and the poisoned animals before we do anything else."

"But how?" Tobin asked, his brow furrowed.

Even if he had felt well, the pangolin could not imagine keeping up with the glowers. "We'll never catch up if we follow them—they're moving too fast!"

"We're not going to follow them," said the fox, with a small smile. "I know where that plateau is… and better yet, I know a shortcut. We're not going to let those star creatures beat us again. This time, we're getting there first."

Chapter Sixteen
THE RACE

"Come on, *amigo*! Quit stallin' and keep clawin'!" Bismark shouted. "We need to get there before those glowers destroy all our precious flowers!"

Dawn led the way while the glider sailed through the overcast sky above. Tobin, however, was struggling once again. The ground was quickly growing rough, and a sharp rock scratched his paw, piercing a layer of skin. Bismark turned to see the pangolin stumble and drop.

"Ouch! Oh, Bismark, it's not so easy when you

have to walk! I've never felt earth this crunchy and hard!" Tobin cried. The burning poison in his stomach was now accompanied by a sharp pain in his foot. *Could he continue?* he wondered. *Would he make it? What if they didn't reach the flowers in time?* The pangolin's thoughts turned to the woylies. *Would he end up like their friend Dewey?* Tobin paused, breathless and panicked. But then, Bismark's familiar cry rang through the air.

"*Mon dieu*, what is this terrible terrain?" he exclaimed, settling to the ground with a flap of his flaps. "My lady, my light, my love—where the heavens are you taking us?"

Jarred from his thoughts and fears, Tobin took a deep breath. Then he scanned his surroundings.

The Brigade had entered an unfamiliar region of gravel and sand. As far as the eye could see, there was nothing but hard, dry earth and a few prickly cactus. Tangles of dried, gray grass whispered and tumbled through a cold wind.

Dawn's red fur stood on end, shielding her skin from the chill. This was a far cry from the rich land and humid forest of their valley, but she knew it was the right way. It had to be. "Come on," she urged. "Just a little bit farther."

Dawn picked her way across the stony landscape, sniffing at the dry earth. A ball of pale, hairy tumbleweed bounced past her and then disappeared into the darkness. The fox took a sudden step after it, further into the desert. Then she hesitated—and took a step back.

Bismark and Tobin looked at one another, their glance clouded with uncertainty.

"Um, 'just a little bit farther,' you said, *correctomundo*?" asked the sugar glider. "You're…you're not lost, are you, my lovely leader, my tawny trailblazer, my *bella* guide?"

"I'm not lost," said Dawn. But her voice did not carry its usual confidence. The dim, clouded light and the chilly breeze were warping her sense of direction, and she began to wonder if she remembered the shortcut correctly. Had she taken the wrong path? Did she just destroy their chance to reach the blue flowers first? What if the flower field atop the plateau held the last of the flowers?

The fox swallowed hard, attempting to loosen the knot in her chest.

But then, the wind began to die down, and the full moon burst through the clouds. The landscape grew brighter. More familiar.

Dawn turned to take in her surroundings again in the new light.

Then she saw it: in the distance was a small slope …that led up to a flat plain of land.

Tobin followed his leader's gaze. "The plateau!" he breathed.

The corners of Dawn's mouth curled up. "Yes." She nodded.

With renewed energy, the pangolin ran along the path toward the plateau, scrambling up its sloped side. When he reached the top, he was so excited, he nearly leaped into the air. "Dawn, Bismark—hurry!" he called. "You have to see this!"

His two friends raced up the slope behind him. And then, side-by-side, the trio took in the magnificent sight before them.

The plateau's flat surface was completely covered in blue flowers. Each one was healthy and beautiful, fluttering in the breeze, leaves glinting like opals, blue petals shimmering beneath the light of the full moon.

"Oh goodness, we did it!" Tobin said. "We beat the star creatures! I'll finally be okay! Everyone will be healed!"

"You're right, Tobin," said Dawn. The fox inhaled, taking in the fresh, sweet scent of the blossoms. "There are enough flowers here to save the whole valley!"

Their faces brightened in the moonlight as they watched the flowers sway in the night air.

And then...

Thunk.

The Brigade blinked. One of the flowers had vanished, just like the ones in the last field.

Thunk.

Then another.

Thunk.

And another. As each one disappeared, a shining beam of blue light shone up from underground.

Thunk. Thunk. Thunk.

Three more flowers vanished into the earth, causing the ground to glow brighter.

Thunk. Thunk. Thunk.

Thunk. Thunk. Thunk.

"*Oh mon dieu!*" exclaimed Bismark. "The invaders—they're here!"

Dawn shot forward into the field. "Hurry!" she yelled. "Save as many flowers as you can!"

Chapter Seventeen
THE FINAL FLOWER

"This is it, *amigos*! Time to beat those blossom-banditos once and for all! *En garde!*" Bismark shouted.

The sugar glider raced into the field. With each step he took, more flowers vanished underground. They disappeared with alarming speed—leaving nothing behind but holes. And with each new opening formed in the earth's surface, a new beam of eerie blue light shot toward the sky.

"*Hiii-ya*! Let's see you take this one from my unbreakable grasp, moonies!" Bismark cried, lunging toward one of the plants and gripping it tightly around the stalk.

Thunk!

With a sudden jerk, the flower whistled through Bismark's paws and into the earth. The force of its pull rocketed him to the ground and gave him a faceful of dirt.

"*Ach!*" the glider spat. He scrambled to brush off his flaps and reach for another bloom. "Why don't you try this one instead, you wretched flower-filchers!" But just as he wrapped his fingers around a different plant, it, too, was yanked from his clutches.

Thunk!
Thunk!
Thunk!

All across the field, the flowers were disappearing faster than the three friends could react. The plateau was starting to look as barren as the surrounding desert.

"Oh goodness! They're getting them all!" Tobin said in a panic. He tore across the ground, snatching about here and there with his long, blade-like claws. But when he finally managed to get a hold of a flower, he unwittingly snipped its petaled head right off. It tumbled into one of the holes, briefly blocking out the blue light glowing underneath. Then it, too, disappeared from sight.

"*Mon dieu*! It's a melee, a massacre, a moon-slaughter!" Bismark cried. The glider was racing deeper into the field, bolting from flower to flower, but they were slithering into the ground faster than worms down a kiwi bird's gullet.

"Try to keep up with them!" Dawn shouted, but even she, the strongest and swiftest of the trio, could not manage to catch a single blossom before it slipped away. With all the beams of blue light shining from underground, it was getting harder and harder to see clearly and to keep track of the remaining flowers.

"They're everywhere, *mes amis*! We're surrounded and we can't even see our surrounders!" cried Bismark, stomping his small paws on the ground. "We'll never catch up with these crazy critters while they're down there!"

"Bismark, that's it! We need to stop them at the source!" shouted Dawn. With a quick pivot and dive, she lunged at the beam of light shooting up from one of the mounds and began to dig furiously. The pangolin immediately followed, digging with his long, curved claws, but their efforts were too late. The beams of light faded from sight, and the two friends came up with nothing but paws filled with dirt.

"What are we going to do?" Tobin cried. The pangolin gazed up from the pile of freshly dug earth and watched in dismay as the few remaining flowers began to shoot underground.

Thunk!

Thunk!

Thunk! Thunk! Thunk!

The beams of light were coming up faster now. Before Tobin and Dawn could even straighten their backs, the last line of flowers had already been zipped away. Only one last blossom remained. It was set slightly apart from the rest, right on the edge of the plateau.

"*Pangolino*! We need that flower for you!" Bismark cried, raising his flaps in the air.

"Oh my, we'll never get there in time!" Tobin cried, his legs and feet wobbling as he tried to regain his balance.

Dawn took a sudden leap but then stopped. She knew she would never be fast enough to reach the blossom before the star creatures. Her amber eyes flickered desperately across the field, searching for a solution. And then she saw the Brigade's final hope.

"Bismark!" she cried.

The sugar glider was standing, his flaps still raised in the air.

"It's up to you now!" Dawn shouted. "You know what this calls for!"

"By all that glides! How long I've yearned to hear those words from your fine, foxy lips!" Bismark cried. Then, with a dramatic swivel, the glider took off running, his tiny fists beating against his chest. "This calls for the...!" But suddenly, something slipped from under his flaps and bounced down in front of him. The sugar glider skidded to an abrupt halt.

"*Mon dieu!*" he gasped. "The magic berry I snagged from those lemurs! If I eat this, I'd be sure to zip to that final flower in no time." His eyes flickered as he imagined his unworldly speed. "But *uno momento...*" he murmured. Slowly, the glider's face fell and his brow crumpled with disappointment. "I wanted to use this fantastical fruit for fun, not fighting! For my own personal pleasure! To glorify my already glorious self!" Bismark stared at the berry in one paw and scratched at his scalp with the other, overcome with conflict. "What should I do?"

Tobin gaped at his frozen friend. "Oh goodness, Dawn, we have to do something!" he cried. And then, without another word—without even thinking—the pangolin curled into a ball and rolled in front of the fox's paws. The fox knew exactly what Tobin had in mind. She reeled back her leg and gave him a mighty kick.

Through the air, in the safety of his armored ball, Tobin flew: past Bismark, over the mounds, and toward the plateau's sharp edge. Then, with a bounce and a leap, the pangolin landed, uncurled his body, and dug his claws into the ground so he wouldn't fall off the edge.

For a moment, he paused, getting his bearings. Then he spotted it: the final flower. At once, he shot out his long, sticky tongue, and wrapped it around the flower's long stem.

But when he yanked it, he felt a strong force pulling the flower back underground.

"Hehp!" Tobin lisped. "The sthar creathures! They've got the fwower by the rooth!" The pangolin dug his heels into the earth, but the strength of the glower's pull dragged the stem into the ground bit by bit.

"I've got you!" It was Dawn. She had clambered up behind her friend and wrapped her paws around his scaly body. Then she, too, dug her heels in the dirt, transforming herself into an anchor. But still, the flower's head was inching closer and closer to the ground.

"Oh *mon dieu*, what a shame...." Bismark sighed, his mouth forming a mischievous grin. "It appears there's no time to eat the berry after all!" Quickly, he tucked the red fruit back in his flap before scurrying behind his companions and pulling with all his miniscule might.

The flower's stem was stretching under the stress of all the tugging. Back and forth. Back and forth. And neither side seemed to show signs of defeat. At one moment, the Brigade was dragged almost to the earth themselves. And at the next, they nearly succeeded in pulling the flower out to its roots.

"*Mon dieu*, I don't know how much more of this terrible tug-of-war I can take!" Bismark said. "Even my massive muscles have their limit!"

Through clenched teeth, Dawn growled her instructions. "Hold fast, both of you! One last pull, on my mark!" she said. She took a deep breath. "One…two …three!"

With a mighty, unified heave, Tobin rolled his body, Bismark beat his flaps, and Dawn wrenched her head.

Plink!

Suddenly, the plant felt weightless in their grasp. The three friends tumbled down together in a heap, the flower coming up and falling before them. Bismark bumped his head as he landed face-first in the dirt.

"Oh goodneth, we did it!" cried Tobin. The

pangolin uncurled himself and reeled the blue flower in with his tongue, prepared to eat it at last.

"*Uno momento, pangolino!*" called Bismark, scrambling to his feet. "Perhaps we should share that final blossom. Might help with my swelling, as well." Bismark rubbed at the small bump that was forming right on his bald spot.

"Bismark!" Dawn scolded. "Eat the flower, Tobin," she instructed. "*All* of it."

The pangolin obeyed at once.

"Right, *si*, it's—it's for you," Bismark stammered, brushing the dirt off his coat. "I was kidding, of course. What's a bumpy noggin compared to a poisoned belly?" Bismark flapped toward Dawn. "Plus," he added, "even with my wound, I am still horribly handsome. Isn't that right, my love?"

Dawn looked at the pangolin. Already, his gaze seemed more steady. "You'll be all right now," she said.

"Yes," agreed Bismark. He threw his arm around his scaly friend, and the three friends stood in a huddle, catching their breath and letting the moment sink in.

Dawn smiled at Tobin. With the pangolin cured, the Brigade felt strong and complete. And they were capable of accomplishing anything together: curing the animals, defeating the star creatures, and confronting Iris. No matter how long, difficult, and dangerous their mission, they would succeed. Everything would be okay.

"*Oh mon dieu!*" Bismark's high-pitched yelp rang through the night.

Startled, Tobin and Dawn jumped. Then they followed the line of the sugar glider's bulging eyes and his shaky flap pointing over the plateau's edge.

A crowd was approaching, climbing over the field's edges from all sides. A swarm of creatures…their movements stiff yet quick, their pupils wild and wide.

"It's the lemurs!" cried Tobin.

"How did they find us?" asked Bismark, clutching Dawn's tawny leg.

Dawn narrowed her eyes. "Iris must have sent them here to make sure all the flowers had been taken," she said.

"*Aye, aye, aye-aye,*" the lemurs were chanting again.

The lemurs caught sight of the Brigade and a wave of excitement rolled through the crowd. Their fur stood on edge as they closed in on the trio.

"*Mon dieu!*" Bismark cried. "Looks like our brilliant Brigade was in the wrong place at the right time.

I mean, the right place at the wrong time. I mean…"

"*Aye, aye, aye-aye! Aye, aye, aye-aye!*"

The lemurs were in a frenzy now, moving faster and faster, arms extended toward the Brigade.

"D-Dawn?" Tobin yelped. "What do we do!?"

Dawn's eyes darted across the landscape, searching for some sort of escape route. But there was nowhere to go—the lemurs had stretched their pack into a circle around the Brigade. Dawn, Tobin, and Bismark were completely surrounded by the chanting, menacing crowd.

"There has to be a way," the fox muttered.

"*Bien sûr,* there's a way, my sweet!" Bismark said. "We bolt straight ahead, ram them down, dodge …their…clutches!" He punched a fist in the air, but his voice faded.

"*Aye, aye, aye-aye! Aye, aye, aye-aye!*" The lemurs' chanting grew even louder and their circle drew even tighter. They were now standing shoulder-to-shoulder, leaving no room between them. And the circle was thick and solid—at least ten rows deep all around.

Dawn shook her head. Even if she agreed with her friend's rash approach, it would never work. The Brigade was outplayed and greatly outnumbered.

Dawn opened her mouth, searching for a command, or at least words of comfort or wisdom. But there was nothing to say. The lemurs were nearly touching them now.

The Brigade was caught.

Chapter Eighteen
THE CAPTIVES

"This is an outrage! Release us at once, you traitors!" yelled Bismark. "I'll flap you silly for this!"

The sugar glider wriggled and squirmed, but his efforts were useless. The lemurs held strong, ignoring Bismark's cries, and marched onward, pushing and tugging the Brigade along with them.

"Where are they taking us?" Tobin yelped. The pangolin struggled to catch a glimpse of his surroundings, but all he could see besides a mass of brown fur was the blur of the treetops above. "Hello?" he asked, attempting to communicate with his captors. "Excuse me?"

But the lemurs did not reply. They simply marched onward, eyes blank and grips tight. As the branches overhead became thicker and the crunch of leaves became louder under the lemurs' paws, the animals chanted even louder than before:

"*Aye...aye...aye-aye.*"

"*Aye...aye...aye-aye.*"

Dawn's jaw tightened. "I think that's your answer, Tobin."

"They're taking us to the aye-aye? *Oh mon dieu,* we are doomed!" Bismark screeched. "I cannot go back to that malodorous *muchacha.* Who knows what she'll do when she gets her hideous hands on us! Pulverize us with her pointers, grate us with her grinders, soufflé us for a star-creature snack?"

Suddenly, the lemurs came to a halt. Dawn's fur stood on end as the captors ceased their chanting. She recognized something in the air—a burning smell. Something gritty, or maybe metallic.

But before Dawn could identify the odor, the lemurs released their hold on the Brigade, letting them fall to the ground in a heap.

"Oof! How about a little warning before you so

roughly handle my delicate yet masculine physique?" Bismark grumbled, wiping the dirt from his eyes.

Lying curled on the ground, Tobin cradled his stomach and moaned. The blue flower had worked—the terrible burning was gone—but he remained queasy, as though the plant and the poison were still battling it out in his belly. And the lemurs' less-than-gentle handling certainly hadn't helped the pain.

Tobin took a determined breath and struggled to his feet. Then he coughed and squinted through the thick dust that surrounded him. "Where are we?" he asked.

Dawn sniffed the charred air and looked down at her paws. The ground was burned and marked with small holes. We've been here before, thought the fox. She spun, dragging her tail through the ash. Then she saw it: the star stone. And standing on top of it—ragged, yet triumphant—was none other than Aye-Aye Iris.

"Well, well, well. Look what we have here." The aye-aye's familiar, scratchy voice cut through the dense air. The words were punctuated by a loud, happy cackle.

"You have done well, my lemurs," she continued, turning to the furry primates. Despite the swirling dust, the lemurs stood motionless and unblinking, glued to Iris's mesmerizing gaze.

"*Aye, aye, aye-aye!*" they chanted. "*Aye, aye, aye-aye!*"

Frantically, Dawn searched through the crowd. Everything—everyone—was connected: Iris, the lemurs, the aliens. She was sure the blue glow would appear any moment now. The fox waited, bracing herself for its arrival. But nothing came—the night remained dusty and dim.

Dawn gave a small sigh of relief. The Brigade had enough to battle without the star creatures. She looked back at Iris.

The aye-aye still stared down at the lemurs, but now her hand was raised overhead. The fox watched as, with a single finger, Iris drew a semi-circle in the air. As though caught in a spell, the lemurs responded by forming a single-file line and creating an arc around the Brigade.

Iris cackled at her three captives. "The ones too smart to join Aye-Aye Iris," Iris snickered, exposing her dark, yellow teeth. "Look where that's gotten you now!"

"*Mon dieu*–you traitor! Double-crosser! Back-stabber!" Bismark shouted, pointing an accusing flap at the aye-aye. "You may be a lemur, but you act like a rat!"

Iris's big orange eyes flickered mischievously.

Then she reached under her armpit and fished through a tangled tuft of fur. When she pulled out her hand, a flower, its blue petals and orange center glowing like jewels, twirled in her long fingers.

Bismark's eyes bulged. Dawn released a low growl.

"Oh goodness, Iris! You have one with you right now?" Tobin cried.

"Yes," she hissed. "And only Aye-Aye Iris knows where she hid all the rest!" With a smirk, Iris tore the blue petals from the stalk and tossed them over her head. They showered over her as she bent back with a cackle.

"Oh goodness, what are you doing?" gasped Tobin. "Don't you know how many animals need that?"

"Of course Aye-Aye knows," the lemur snapped. She slid from the stone with a rustle and landed before the Brigade. "Aye-Aye Iris knows all. She warned you, remember?" she asked, drawing closer. "She offered you information, wisdom, protection. But you didn't listen."

"Why are you doing this?" Dawn demanded, narrowing her eyes at the aye-aye. "Why are you working with the invaders? Why are you leading them?" The fox raised her voice louder. "What do they want? What do *you* want?"

Iris shook her head, stringy fur whipping over her face. Then she pointed one of her long, bony fingers at the Brigade. "You didn't listen!" she snapped.

Dawn growled and crouched down low, poised to attack, but before she could, the aye-aye raised her finger and clucked disapprovingly. "What do you think you're doing, fox?" she snarled. She gestured toward the other lemurs with her claws. They took a menacing step forward, and Dawn backed down. She and her friends were far too outnumbered to launch an attack.

Satisfied with the retreat, Aye-Aye Iris slowly lowered her finger. "No, you didn't listen," she repeated, muttering under her breath. "No one listened!" she screamed. "No one ever listens! But that's about to change. Oh, yes. They'll listen to Aye-Aye Iris now!"

The aye-aye turned wildly to face the Brigade, her eyes burning with rage, her whole body shaking. Then she centered her gaze on Bismark.

"*Mon dieu*, the loco one is staring right at me!" he cried, shielding himself with his flaps. "I know I'm attractive, but please, find someone else to ogle! Try the scaly one!"

Iris clenched her hands into tight fists. "*Loco*? Crazy? Yes, of course that's what you think!" she screamed. "That's what they all say! 'Stay away from the aye-aye! Don't talk to Iris! Don't go anywhere close!'"

"Oh goodness! We're sorry!" cried Tobin. He eyed the fallen petals that lay at the aye-aye's feet. "Just don't destroy any more flowers!"

Iris's leathery ears twitched in their sockets and she licked her dry, cracked lips with her tongue. "Destroy?" she asked with a snort. "Oh no. I would never do that. These flowers are Aye-Aye Iris's secret— her power! As long as she has these, everyone will depend on her. They'll want to come to the aye-aye. They'll need to come to see Iris!"

"Iris, stop! There's no time for this—animals' lives are at stake!" Dawn shouted.

"Enough!" the lemur screamed. She spun around, let out a shrill, piercing whistle, and the lemurs stepped toward her in unison. Then Iris began to wave her long, bony fourth fingers before their eyes like a pendulum.

"Aye, aye, aye-aye," she muttered.

"*Aye, aye, aye-aye!*" they chanted.

"Lemurs, dig!" the aye-aye commanded.

In a flash, the army of lemurs began clawing at the dusty earth beneath their feet. Their limbs churned up the dirt with incredible speed, creating a pit that grew deeper and deeper within moments.

Dawn stared at the lemurs: why were they doing this? Why were they listening to the aye-aye? She stared at the lemurs, moving as fast as lightning, but with no emotion and empty eyes. Then she looked at the aye-aye who was totally still but for her swaying fingers.

Back and forth, back and forth, swayed the aye-aye's fingers.

Left, right, left, right, moved the lemurs' eyes.

The fox's jaw fell open in sudden comprehension. At last, it all made sense. "A trance." Her eyes were fixed on the aye-aye's finger. "That's how she gets them to do what she wants! That's how she's controlling them!"

Tobin, too, stared at the rhythmic, mesmerizing motion of the aye-aye's fingers. "Oh goodness! Is...is that what she's going to do to us?" he cried. "Take over our minds?" The pangolin quickly turned away from Iris and curled into a ball.

Her ears flinching, Iris glanced at the pangolin without slowing her fingers. "Oh no," she whispered. Her mouth spread into a ragged grin. "Aye-Aye Iris has something different planned for you. You three—the Nocturnal Brigade, as they call you—know too much. Aye-Aye Iris cannot risk you revealing her brilliant plan to the others." The aye-aye snapped her gaze back to the lemurs. The hole they were digging was very deep now. Dangerously deep.

"Lemurs! Take them to the pit!" Iris shrieked.

Dawn snarled, Tobin clutched himself tightly, and Bismark extended his flaps, but it was no use. The lemurs were too fast, too many, and the Brigade went hurtling down, down, down to the bottom of the freshly dug pit.

Chapter Nineteen
ALIENS

The three friends landed at the bottom of the pit in a heap. Then, slowly, they staggered to their feet.

Tobin rubbed his sore scales and looked around frantically, desperate to find a way out. The lemurs, with their crazed energy, had managed to dig a massive hole— as big as a beluga whale's stomach. The moonlight shone down through the pit's wide mouth overhead, but even with its pale, familiar light, it felt as if the Brigade had been swallowed whole. The pit was vast, its walls, high and steep. Escape seemed completely impossible.

"Oh goodness," Tobin gasped. "We're trapped!"

Desperately, Dawn circled the pit, searching in vain for a foothold in its walls. She tried digging into ground, but the dirt was densely packed—it would take ages to burrow out. Even Tobin's sharp claws would barely make a dent in the earth.

She growled in frustration. "We have to find a way out," she said, looking to her friends. Her eyes darted back and forth between them. *"Think! What can we do?"*

"Worry not, my love," Bismark said with a chuckle. "This is *pas de problème* for we flappy folk. Now please, *por favor:* watch, observe, and be awed!" The glider took a deep breath, puffed out his chest, and shot a wink at the fox. Then, taking a running start, he began to furiously wave his flaps. But it was no use. Bismark barely lifted off the ground, and, before he knew it— *SPLAT!*—he'd smacked face-first into the pit's rock-hard wall.

Tobin watched his over-confident friend crumple into a heap on the ground. "Oh goodness, Bismark, are you okay?" The pangolin nudged the sugar glider's side with his snout.

"*Si,* yes, of course I'm okay! What kind of

question is that, *pangolino*?" Bismark sputtered, and scrambled to his feet. "I can foil any foe, vanquish any vermin, attack any atrocious aye-aye—" the sugar glider spat out some dirt and used a wad of saliva to polish his fur "—as soon as my flaps are clean." He sputtered and polished again. "Ah yes, there we go. Good as—"

Suddenly, a loud cackle rang out from overhead. The sugar glider's mouth snapped shut and he looked up. Aye-Aye Iris leaned over the rim of the pit, finger raised, malice burning in her wild eyes. "Lemurs!" she screeched, waving her long, bony fingers. "Fill the pit!"

"*Quoi*? What new crazy command is this? You've already filled the pit—with us!" Bismark cried. But before he could say another word, the sugar glider was hit square in the face with a clod of dirt. The hypnotized lemurs had begun shoveling large clumps of soil down on the Brigade.

"Oh goodness, they're burying us alive!" Tobin cried, protecting his head with his claws as the earth rained down across his scales.

Bismark's small chest began to heave. "*Oh mon dieu…* my worst dream is becoming reality," he gasped. "I shall die with a soiled coat!"

Dawn's brow creased with despair. The lemurs' paws moved in a frenzied blur. Despite the pit's considerable size, the dirt was already covering her feet ...and it was nearly up to Bismark's waist.

As the fox's mind raced, Bismark's voice interrupted her thoughts. "*Pah*! The sugar glider was not meant for this sort of filth! This humiliating work!" In an attempt to stay clean, he shoveled flapfuls of dirt to the side. But his efforts were endless and useless: the dirt kept raining down, Bismark kept shoveling it away, and the ground just kept growing higher and higher.

Dawn growled and watched her friend shriek as another clod of earth splattered at his feet. Bismark leaped atop his tidy dirt mound in shock then shook his tiny fist at the lemurs.

And that's when it hit her. The fox's eyes widened. "Bismark, that's it!" she cried.

At once, the fox raced to the sugar glider's side and began to pack the newly dug soil so it would support her weight, too. "Tobin, Bismark, follow my lead! We can use all this dirt to our advantage and build our way out!"

With Dawn at the helm, the three friends shaped the falling soil into a ramp that would lead above ground. Tobin worked eagerly. The plan was a good one. Soon they would be free! But then, a *tap tap tap* caught his attention. The pangolin froze.

"Listen!" Tobin whispered. "Did you hear that?"

Dawn and Bismark paused and raised their ears. At first, they could hear nothing through the shower of dirt hurled by the lemurs. But then, they heard it, echoing down into the pit:

Tap. Tap. Tap.

Slowly, shielding their eyes from the falling debris, the Brigade-mates gazed up. Iris was staring at them, crouched on her haunches, her long, bony finger tapping at the pit's rim.

Tap. Tap. Tap.

"*Oh mon dieu*, I can't take this torture anymore!" Bismark shuddered. "We're trapped, we're dirty, and now we have to hear that terrible tapping again?"

Tap. Tap. Tap.

Dawn's mind started to spin. Why was Iris tapping again? What was she doing? The fox stared into Iris's eyes. Then, suddenly, her chest tightened and she spun toward her friends. "Everyone, quick!" she shouted. "Prepare to—"

Before Dawn could finish, another noise echoed through the pit's depths. But this time it wasn't Iris's fingernail. Instead, it was a faint *click, click, click.* And it was coming from the pit's walls.

Click. Click. Click.

Suddenly, the lemurs stopped shoveling dirt in to the pit. The sugar glider's brown eyes widened.

Click. Click. Click.

The sound was growing louder now, faster.

Click, click, click!

All at once, the pit's walls began to tremble. Crumbs of dirt began to flake from the sides. The Brigade's pile collapsed beneath their feet, and Iris let out an ear-piercing cackle. Then...

CLACK!

With a sudden flash, narrow tunnels opened in the walls—and blinding beams of blue light shot through them, into the pit. "It's the star creatures!" cried Tobin. "They're here!"

Chapter Twenty
THE STAR CREATURES, ILLUMINATED

"*Oh mon dieu*, this is the end! Clicked to death by the faceless fiends from outer space!" Bismark screamed as the invaders swarmed into the pit from all sides. "We're surrounded, mes amis! Quick, Dawn, hold me close for our final good-byes!" Bismark sobbed into the fox's fur.

CLICK, CLICK, CLICK!

Dawn cringed as the glowers' noise grew louder

and sharper. The pit, lit only by the moon just moments ago, now shone brightly with hundreds of beams of blue light.

Tobin stared, aghast, at the light. Beneath the creatures' eerie, blue glow, he thought he saw claws again …or, wait, maybe they were huge fangs. Whatever they were, they looked powerful enough to lop off his tail with a single swipe.

"Stop right there you ghastly glowers, you awful aliens, you foreign freaks!" Bismark yelped, tearing himself from Dawn's haunches and waving his flaps like a maniac. "Do not take another…I don't know…step? Jump? Moonbeam slide?" The sugar glider scrunched his face in confusion. "Pah! Who knows how you star creatures tango. But you catch my drift: stop this attack this instant!"

The invaders, however, paid Bismark no heed. In fact, they appeared to be moving even faster now, drawing closer to the trio with every passing moment.

"Oh goodness!" gasped Tobin. As the invaders approached, the pangolin saw something scarier than any claws or fangs. The star creatures appeared to have many eyes gleaming from their alien heads. Round, shiny, winking, blinking eyes. Tobin cowered in his scales and his stomach lurched. How many eyes did each creature have? Six? Eight? Ten? He couldn't tell. And what kind of power, he wondered, did all those eyes have? Could they zap him? Fry him? End him with a single glare? "What should we do?" Tobin yelped.

With his body trembling and his insides forming a huge, hard knot, the pangolin swiveled his scaly neck from one friend to the other. Bismark cowered behind his flaps. And even Dawn, though she stood perfectly still, betrayed a glimmer of fear in her eyes.

Click, click, click.

Click! Click! Click!

The glowers were drawing even nearer now— just a few tail lengths away.

"Help! Help!" The glider shrieked and clutched Dawn's hind leg once more. "Oh, you monsters, why don't you go back to your own planet where you belong!"

Click, click, click!

Click, click, click!

Tobin gulped. The invaders were close enough to touch now. And new ones continued to pour through the holes in the walls. There were so many—more than hundreds! Thousands! With tens of thousands of eyes! The creatures' clicking grew louder, deafening. Their glow grew brighter and brighter. The pangolin felt his stomach twist and writhe and churn.

"Somebody help *meeeeeeee*!" Bismark wailed. He was completely fastened to Dawn now, all four of his miniscule limbs wrapped tightly around her leg. "They're going to kill me! Zip me! Zap me! Zoom me straight into space!" His yelps grew louder. "This is it! The *grande finale!* Death!"

The sugar glider wiped his wet face on Dawn's rust-colored fur, burying his cheek in its folds. "Oh, Dawn, light of my life, fire of my flaps, my sweet, my soul! I must profess my love to you in every tongue, in every language I know! *Je t'aime. Ti amo. Yo...te...ti, tu, toi, Quoi!?* I cannot remember the others. Even my words are lost! This is the end! All is over! Oh, for the lift of my flaps—" Bismark gazed up pleadingly at the night sky, preparing to beg the heavens for help...but then he paused. Where were the stars? Where was the moon?

"*Dios mio! Quelle horreur!* Dawn, *mi amore,* my sweet—we are departing this earth...and we can't even enjoy the romance of the full moon in our final moments!"

The fox looked up. Indeed, the moon had

retreated fully behind the clouds, as if it, too, were fearful of the star creatures. The sky was gray, and the entire universe felt suddenly barren, lifeless, and dull.

Dawn shifted her nervous gaze back to the invaders. But now, somehow, there was no glow in sight. From the time she'd looked up to the time she'd looked down, the glowers had completely vanished!

"Dawn...what's happening?" uttered Tobin, squinting in the flat, black air.

The fox remained silent and blinked hard, trying to adjust to the sudden darkness. She narrowed her eyes to focus. Then her amber eyes widened and the hair along her back pricked on end. She drew in a sharp breath and recoiled.

The Brigade was not alone. In fact, they remained fully surrounded. But the creatures with them in the pit were no longer aglow. The fox's mouth went dry as she studied them. Without their sharp blue light, she could see them clearly now—their two pincer claws, their six spindly legs, their eight beady eyes.

Tobin had covered his face with his armored tail, but slowly lowered it to peek at the creatures. Row after row of them stood before him, with all of their eyes fixed on the Brigade.

"Oh my goodness, where are the glowers?" he asked. "And who are *they*!?"

Bismark gasped, confused as well. "*Uno momento!* Where did the star creatures go? Are they invisible? Are they above us? Below us? *Inside* us!?" The sugar glider froze in terror.

Dawn's gaze shot up to the opening of the pit, where the clouds were beginning to part, slowly revealing the full moon once again. Dawn looked at the creatures again. This time, in the partial moonlight, the aliens looked somewhat...*familiar.*

The fox moved closer to them and stared hard. They were strange looking, yes, but aliens, no. These beings weren't creatures from a distant star. These beings were from this world!

"Scorpions!" she cried.

The creatures moved toward Bismark and started to glow again, transforming before his very eyes.

"How is this possible?" Bismark screeched. "Aliens who have the power to look like earthlings? What evil magic is this?"

"They don't *look* like earthlings," Dawn said through clenched teeth. "They *are* earthlings. They are scorpions," she repeated. The fox's gaze traced the mass of creatures, who, once again, shone with their eerie, blue glow. "I'd always heard they glow in moonlight, but I'd never seen it with my own eyes because they spend most of their lives underground."

Dawn nodded as all suddenly became clear. "Now I understand why there are so many mounds," she said. "When the fallen star hit the earth, it disturbed the scorpions, and they all surfaced. It's all making sense now...."

"But if these little buggers are from the forest, why are they attacking us?" Bismark cried, throwing his flaps in the air. "What do you want, you scuttling scoundrels? What are you doing with that appalling aye-aye?"

The scorpions did not reply. Nor did they stand down. Instead, they continued to click their pincers and draw in toward the Brigade.

"Um, *hola*? Comrades? Forest friends?" said Bismark. "Maybe you don't know who you're talking to after living underground for so long. I am Bismark, god amongst gliders, and we are the Nocturnal Brigade, heroes amongst all! Don't you know how to treat your friends, your leaders, your—"

The fox placed a paw over her friend's mouth, muffling the rest of his words. "Quiet, Bismark!" she ordered. "Scorpions are earthlings, but they're also poisonous. Poisonous and deadly." She narrowed her amber eyes. "They may not be dangerous star creatures, but I fear they might be even worse."

"Poisonous," Tobin repeated. "So *they're* the ones who ruined the pomelos! They're the ones who made us sick!" The pangolin clutched his stomach. Fear mixed with queasiness was making it rumble and roil.

Dawn nodded. "They must have." She looked at the scorpions' black, beady eyes and sharp, venomous stingers. "Make no mistake about it—these creatures are not friendly."

Tobin, Bismark, and Dawn watched in terror as the scorpions prepared to attack, carefully and precisely arranging themselves in the sharp shape of a triangle, its point aiming right at the Brigade. Then, together, they ever so slowly raised their curved tails above their heads, their stingers dripping with poison.

"Oh goodness, no!" Tobin cried, covering his face once more.

"*Mon dieu*," Bismark wailed. "We *are* doomed!"

Chapter Twenty-One
GEYSERRHEA

Click, click, click!

The scorpions trained their thousands of eyes on the Brigade and let out a loud, menacing *hiss*.

"Oh for the love of the night, for *l'amour de la nuit*! I promise to live my life to the fullest, if only I may live!" Bismark sobbed. "I will glide off the tallest peaks, touch the softest fur, feast upon the sweetest fruit! I will never take anything for granted. Never let the moment pass me by. Just let me live!"

In a sudden blur, one of the glowers darted toward Bismark with a sharp *click* before falling back. The sugar glider let out a terrified yelp and scrambled up Dawn's leg and onto her neck.

Click, click, click.

Hisssssss.

Click, click, click!

Hisssssss!

The scorpions were close enough to touch now, their glow growing brighter and brighter. But then, suddenly, the moonlight above disappeared again, and the creatures' eerie light melted away.

The Brigade looked up: Aye-Aye Iris had reappeared, and her wild, ragged fur cast shadows that darkened the pit to nearly pitch black.

"What are you waiting for!?" she screeched at the scorpions. Her long, bony hands clutched the rim of the pit. "End them!"

"Quick, *mi amore,* look out!" Bismark cried. The sugar glider tugged at the fox's ears as one of the biggest scorpions made a quick jab at her front paws. Dawn jerked back, quickly stepping away, but her rapid movement sent the sugar glider hurtling off her back and high into the air.

"*Oh mon dieu*! You've tossed me straight into the den of death!" Bismark cried, He waved his flaps frantically above the mass of scorpions beneath him, trying to escape them, but it was no use. The glider hovered above the creatures for a moment, then fell directly into the swarm.

"No, no, not *moi*!" Bismark wailed as the scorpions scuttled around to face him. Then the largest, most menacing of the invaders stepped forward and hissed. All eight of its beady eyes flashed with fury. Its body tensed and its stinger arched behind it, poised to strike.

"Bismark!" Tobin screamed. His stomach lurched and a searing pang stung his side. The fear of the moment, the thought of losing Bismark, the last of the poison still in his system—it was all simply too much to bear. His entire body began to convulse, as if he was being torn apart from within.

"*Eurrghhh!*"

The force of it hit him like a boulder. All the pressure that had been building up since he had eaten the blue flower and all the fear he'd felt since his capture had finally reached its peak.

The pangolin squinted his watery eyes.

"Tobin, what's wrong?" Dawn knew Tobin well,

but she'd never known him to make a noise quite like that.

Bismark raised one eyebrow and froze in place, and even the scorpions that surrounded them paused, tails in mid-air, stiffening at Tobin's startling sound.

"Tobin?" Dawn whispered urgently.

The pangolin was sweating now. His entire body was vibrating.

"Tobin! What's wrong?" the fox tried again.

The scorpions began to buzz and click. A few began to clack furiously, and the biggest of the bunch let out a wild hiss. And then, all at once, at the sight of the quivering, quaking, shivering, shaking pangolin, the scorpions started to scatter, scurrying back into the holes from which they'd emerged.

"What's going on down there!?" shrieked the aye-aye. She began striking her gnarled fingernail against the ground in enraged *taps*. "Where do you think you're going? I did not dismiss you!" she screamed. "You haven't finished your job! You haven't—!"

"*Eurrrrgggghh!*"

Tobin's extraordinary, pained grunt came again, and Iris shot him a terrified glance. The pangolin now lay in the center of the pit with legs splayed. His mouth gaped open, then it closed, then opened again. Iris's orange eyes widened in alarm.

The muscles in the pangolin's face tightened and he clenched his jaw. Dawn's heart jumped. She knew that look.

"Aim for the tunnels!" she shouted. "Tobin, back up to the wall!"

Half-sliding, half-crawling, the pangolin eased his way to the pit's wall just in time.

"*Eurrrrgggghh!*" His knotted stomach finally let loose—and with that, his scent glands unclenched.

Torrents of spray shot from him, straight into the underground tunnels. Tobin's pain eased. Then the pressure began to build again...and another wave of spray shot out...and another. With every passing moment, the pangolin felt lighter and lighter, freer and freer, clearer and clearer of the remaining poison that had ravaged his insides for the past few nights. Finally, with one last little toot, he fell from the wall on wobbly legs and squinted up.

For a moment, nothing seemed to have happened. The Brigade stood motionless, alone within the pit.

"Oh, Dawn!" Tobin looked to the fox. "That's ...that's all I've got," he said breathlessly. "I...I don't think your plan worked."

"Just wait," said the fox.

The moon slipped out from behind the clouds, and the trio stared up at it, contemplating their fate. And then...

Whoosh!

Bam!

Blast!

Suddenly, the moonlight was obscured—not by rain clouds, but by clouds of Tobin's powerful, defensive spray! Green clouds of stink exploded up above from the tunnels that the scorpions had dug.

Poof! Poof! Poof!

All across the crater, Iris's hypnotized lemurs were blown off their feet by the stinky geysers of gunk, which shot out of the mounds at their feet like hot springs.

"*Oh mon dieu!*" Bismark cried. "May the moon have mercy. It's geyserrhea!"

Straining to see above the rim, the Brigade could just catch sight of the lemurs fleeing in all directions. But the thick fog of Tobin's spray was making it nearly impossible for them to navigate, and the geysers kept knocking them down left and right.

"Lemurs!" From somewhere in the distance, Iris's voice rang out.

"*Aye...aye....*" The lemurs responded, awaiting

their next command, but the chant had barely passed their lips before another explosion of Tobin's geyserrhea shook the earth and blasted them into oblivion.

The aye-aye let out a terrible squawk then cried out again in desperation: "Aye-Aye Iris commands you to close your noses! She commands you to hold your breath!"

But it was no use. With great blasts of Tobin's gunk shooting out all around, the lemur legion slowly but surely tumbled, unconscious, to the crater's harsh ground.

"No! No! No!" Iris's cry pierced the dark. "You incompetent creatures! Worthless ring-tails! Stupid servile rodents!" The aye-aye ranted and raved, her cracking voice echoing throughout the crater. But then she paused.

"No matter!" she croaked. Her tone evened off. "Aye-Aye Iris doesn't need you anyway. Aye-Aye Iris has won!" The ends of her lips curled up. "Only Aye-Aye Iris knows where all the blue flowers are. Aye-Aye Iris will be needed by everyone. She has the only cure!"

With one final cackle, Iris fled across the crater. Then, with the lemurs unconscious and the aye-aye gone, the night fell quiet.

Tobin and Bismark looked at Dawn.

"Now what?" asked the pangolin, finally recovering from his mighty blast.

Dawn narrowed her eyes and checked the walls of the pit. With Tobin's spray softening the soil, it would now be possible to climb out. "Now we escape," she said, her voice hard with determination. "Now we go get that aye-aye."

Chapter Twenty-Two
BISMARK'S FLIGHT

"*Blech*! Great Scott, *pangolino*, your powerful poofs melted the pit into stinky sludge!" sputtered the sugar glider. Bismark shielded his nose with a flap as he scrambled up the pit's slimy slope. "Your latest explosion is your worst one yet! It nabs the nostrils, thrashes the throat, fouls my fabulous fur!"

Tobin bowed his snout bashfully. "Oh goodness. Well, at least the poison is finally out of my body!" he said shyly.

Dawn nodded.

"*Mais oui*," agreed Bismark. "And I suppose I must thank you, despite all this crud on my coat. *Merci,* my stinky *amigo,* for soiling the soil and saving the night!" With a final leap, the sugar glider surfaced above ground and lifted his flaps victoriously. "Free at last!" he cried.

With a helpful nudge from Dawn, Tobin made his way out of the pit as well. Dawn hoisted herself up after him and scanned the crater. Dozens of lemurs lay motionless, passed out in the muck.

"Oh no," she murmured. She looked around wildly, darting a few steps to one side then circling back. She sniffed the air and muffled a small cough. The oily residue of Tobin's blast was still too strong to catch the scent she was seeking.

"*Quoi, mi amore?* What is it?" asked Bismark, affectionately petting her side. "I know it's stinky up here, but we're free! Show me that foxy grin of yours— we've escaped!"

The fox's eyes narrowed and she took a step toward the crater's outermost edge.

"Yes, Bismark. And Iris might, too, if we don't move quickly." Dawn gestured with her snout across the crater's floor. Tobin and Bismark followed her gaze just in time to see two small glints of orange and the stringy tip of a tail fleeing into the night.

"We need to catch her before she vanishes for good!" said the pangolin.

"Yes! After her...now!" rallied Bismark. At once, the sugar glider spread his arms and half-flapped, half-skittered across the crater's slippery ground. Tobin and Dawn scampered after him.

The Brigade hurried through the crater—but quickly skidded to a halt. Just ahead, a few paw's lengths away, the ground began to alight—with an eerie, blue glow.

Tobin's eyes widened into petrified orbs. "The scorpions!" he cried. "They're back!"

"Do not let them pass!" Iris's scratchy command echoed from the distant, dusty darkness.

With a sudden crackling, the ground erupted with new mounds of soil. Scorpions streamed from the earth until the ground where the Brigade stood was completely aglow with the creatures' eerie illumination.

Click, click, click.

Hissssssss.

"Oh *mon dieu*, don't you glowbugs know when to quit?" Bismark shouted. "Out of the way! We've got a loco *lemur* to catch!"

But the scorpions didn't listen. Instead, they parted to let the biggest, angriest glower scuttle to the head of their group. Bismark's eyes widened. It was the one that had nearly nabbed him in the pit!

"By the stars, he's coming after me again! Do you see this, my love? *Mon ami*? Even the foulest fiends of the underworld cannot resist me!" he cried.

The sugar glider scrambled back, darting away from the poisonous foes. Dawn and Tobin quickly followed, keeping their eyes on the glowers, but the scorpion leader pressed forward, closing in quickly.

"*Dios mio!* Have mercy!" The sugar glider stumbled on the uneven soil and landed in a heap. He cowered, wrapping himself in his flaps as the scorpion raised its tail to strike. "You're making a mistake! You don't want *moi!* Not the innocent, little sugar glider! Not the—"

Bismark peeked out from his flap. The scorpion had disappeared. The glider's eyes widened. "*Mon dieu*, I did it!" he whooped. "Victory is mine! I knew I'd fight my way out of that one!" He took a step toward the other scorpions who had scuttled closer, puffed out his chest, and held up his two scrawny fists. "Now which one of you is next?"

"Dawn! Look out!" The crater echoed with

178

Tobin's sudden cry. The scorpion leader hadn't been after Bismark. Dawn was its target, and it resurfaced from a hole in the ground…right at the fox's feet.

Click, click, click!

"No! Not *mon amour*!" Bismark wailed. "Not my tawny true love!"

The scorpion paid him no heed. Instead, it hissed, arched its body, and aimed its venomous tail. Dawn quickly leaped to the side, evading the sting, but her foot slipped in a puddle of the pangolin's goo and she fell to the ground.

"Oh no! Dawn!" Tobin cried.

The scorpion's eyes gleamed. Its tail shone with a drip of venom. This was it: Dawn was down. A perfect target.

Bismark jumped up in alarm, his arms waving wildly. And then—*plop!*—something slipped from the fold of his flap. The sugar glider's eyes widened and his mouth twisted into a mischievous grin as he picked up the object from the ground.

"Step aside, scorpy!" he yelled. "No one swings their tail at my true love but *moi*!" With a demented whoop, Bismark flapped forward and slid between Dawn and the scorpion. Then he uncurled his fist and revealed the berry he'd taken from the lemurs. "To use in an act of true heroism," he said, beaming, "just as I had always imagined!"

"Bismark, what is that?" asked Tobin. "What are you doing?"

The sugar glider held up the berry, dangling it in front of his mouth.

Dawn's eyes widened in recognition. "Wait, Bismark!" she shouted. "You don't know—"

"Never fear, *mon amour*! If anyone can handle a little sugar, it's *moi*!" the glider cried, and he bit down on the fruit—skin, flesh, pit and all—with a loud crunch.

Everyone stared at Bismark, anxious to see the berry's effect. Even the scorpion could not help but ogle with all eight of its dark, beady eyes.

Watching.

Waiting.

Wondering.

But nothing happened.

Bismark tilted his head from side-to-side in confusion—and then...

"*Mon dieu!*"

Bismark felt his body buzz, tingle, and jump. Then he extended both flaps and shot upward into the night. And so did the scorpion. Bismark had grabbed him right by the tail with his back paws!

Tobin and Dawn stared up at the wild flying creatures, dumbfounded.

"Bismark, drop the scorpion!" Dawn shouted. "Come down!"

But Bismark's only reply was a loud, triumphant battle cry. Despite the scorpion's writhing and twitching, the sugar glider whirled and twirled in the air, his flaps vibrating with such tremendous speed that he was bounding about like a hummingbird.

"Bismark!" Dawn called. "What are you—?"

"Never fear, *mon amour*! This sugar glider was born to fly!" Bismark shouted, and then, angling his flaps to one side, he caught a gust of wind and shot across the crater.

"*Regardez,* everyone!" he cried. "By all that flaps, it's the *true* shooting star of the night!"

Bismark zipped, zoomed, and looped through the air, relishing his newfound speed. The scorpion hissed and snipped, but he dangled helplessly behind. And then, as Bismark hurtled toward the crater's rim, he saw it: a wisp of fur. A gleam of orange. Iris!

"*Oh là là*! So you're not that fast after all, *muchacha*!" Bismark called.

Iris looked wildly toward the skies, her orange eyes first squinting in confusion, then widening in terror.

"Time to say bye-bye, aye-aye!" Bismark shouted. *"Uno...dos...three!"* On his own count, he let go of the squirming scorpion. Down, down, fell the glower: through the air, past the treetops, right toward Iris's scalp. The aye-aye's bony fingers flew up to shield herself, but she was too late.

"Ayeeeeeeeeee!" She let out an ear-splitting shriek as the scorpion's venomous stinger struck the top of her head. Her orange eyes bulged. Then, she desperately spun in a circle until she found the path that led to her cave on the other side of the woods.

"The blue flowers..." she gasped. Iris took a step toward the cave and extended a trembling hand.

But her limbs quickly grew weak and her arm fell back to her side. Her eyes rolled up into her head. And then, in a single, swaying movement, Aye-Aye Iris collapsed to the ground in a small, motionless heap.

Chapter Twenty-Three
THE REAL AYE-AYE IRIS

*T*ap, tap, tap.

Tap, tap, tap.

"Yoo-hoo! Anybody home?" Perched a safe distance away, Bismark was cautiously poking at the motionless aye-aye with a stick.

Up above, the moon had faded, and the sky had shifted from purple to pink. Tobin's mist had cleared in the early morning, leaving the air cool and crisp. For the first time in three nights, the three friends felt nothing but calm and silence as they sat at the base of the fallen star and waited for Iris to stir.

Tap, tap, tap.

Tap, tap, tap.

The sugar glider poked at the aye-aye's shoulder. "Hey, *muchacha*, doesn't this tap-tap-tappy rhythm stir your senses? Wake up already!" When Iris still didn't budge, Bismark aimed the stick at her face and tickled one of her hairy nostrils.

Suddenly, her nose twitched and her jaw extended, circled, and closed, like she was chewing a tough piece of meat. Then she let out a mucousy snort and belched.

Tobin scrunched his face in disgust. Even Dawn lifted an eyebrow and covered her mouth with her tail.

"Oh *mon dieu.*" Bismark rolled his eyes. "Even in rest, she is gruesome, grotesque, *ofensivo* to the soul!" The sugar glider traced his stick down Iris's gangly arm and used it to lift one of her long, black claws. Then, with a sudden jolt, Iris clenched her fist, splintering Bismark's stick. He leaped backward with a yelp.

"Did you see that? The aye-aye's still trying to skewer me!" he shouted, waving the stub of his stick around wildly. "*En garde!*"

Iris opened her two bloodshot eyes. In the dim

light of sunrise, their normally orange blaze had dulled to a lifeless brown, and her hair looked wispy and gray. Slowly, her pupils traced her surroundings, then, with a grunt, she lifted an arm and gestured into the distance. "Lemurs! Oh, my lemurs," she croaked.

The Brigade spun around. The lemurs had recovered from Tobin's powerful spray. There were hundreds of them, and the Brigade gasped at the sight of them all approaching at once.

As they drew closer, the aye-aye's gaze grew more steady, more confident. "I knew you'd come," she whispered, the ends of her lips curling up. "Just in time." Iris gave a faint grin. Then, with her arm still outstretched, she lifted her long, knobby finger and swung it to and fro.

But the lemurs were fixed on the aye-aye's face, not her hand.

"My finger!" called Iris weakly. "Aye-Aye Iris commands you to look at my finger!"

The lemurs did not obey. They had learned her trick, and they shielded their eyes with their paws. The only part of their furry faces left exposed were the defiant, resentful scowls they wore on their mouths.

Iris's eyes darted frantically over the grimacing herd. With her brow twisted in pain and with shaking limbs, she struggled to sit up. "Aye-Aye Iris commands your allegiance!" she called, mustering her strongest voice. "Aye-Aye Iris commands you!"

"They will not obey you," declared Dawn, stepping in front of the aye-aye.

Iris lifted her hands to her head and combed her fingers through her ragged hair. Her orange eyes widened as she felt the welt on her head where the scorpion had stung her. "The poison!" She began to breathe heavily, and her chest rose and fell with panic. "Where are my flowers?" she shrieked. "Someone bring Aye-Aye Iris a flower!"

"The flowers were never yours," Dawn said evenly.

Iris opened her mouth to reply. But then, with a long sigh, she bowed her head and clutched her hands to her heart. When she looked back up at the fox, her dull orange eyes shone with dampness. "You...you don't understand...Aye-Aye Iris..." she began. "She...she's going to...die."

Bismark lifted a flap to his forehead and rolled his bulbous eyes. "*Mon dieu,*" he sighed. "So dramatic! I know I may *look* large and ferocious,"—he paused to flex his scrawny muscles—"but this marsupial isn't a murderer!"

Iris twisted her neck in confusion.

"We found the blue flowers in the cave and gave them out while you slept," Tobin explained, taking a step toward the aye-aye. "Look." The pangolin smiled and gestured out. Iris followed the line of his claw. Circling the rim of the crater were the woylies, bandicoots, kangaroos, and bilbies. Each and every one of them looked healthy. Cured. "We gave them to everyone," Tobin said, "including *you.*"

"*Si,*" confirmed Bismark. "Popped one right in your mouth—your *drooling* mouth—while you snored."

Iris's jaw fell slack. "I…I—"

"You didn't deserve one!" An angry shout rose from the circle of lemurs, cutting off the aye-aye.

Another voice rang out from the lemurs: "You controlled us! *Used* us!"

The group murmured in agreement. Then they drew in, closer and closer to Iris, until they were crowded around her.

"You're dangerous!"

"Devious!"

"Delirious!"

Iris groaned and shrank in upon herself as the lemurs continued to clamor around her. Soon, all the lemurs were joining in the fray.

"Enough." Dawn's voice brought the animals to attention. "This rage will get us nowhere. What we want is an explanation."

Reluctantly, the lemurs backed off, and the aye-aye began to stir. A flash of anger crossed her face. But then it passed, and she slumped back into the dirt and sighed.

"It's no use," she croaked. "These attacks, this hate. It's all Aye-Aye Iris has known." Iris sighed. "No matter what she does to help, no matter what she says, no one believes her. Animals look at Iris and think she's crazy. All anyone can see are her weird long fingers, her ugly orange eyes, her strange crooked teeth." The aye-aye's gaze fell to the ground. "No one sees the *real* Iris."

"Hold up just a tic, *muchacha*," said Bismark. "You did all this because you want a makeover? Why not just clip your nails, trim that fur? No need to go all *cucaracha* on us and team up with those sinister scorpions!" His eyes narrowed. "By the way, I know those evil critters disappeared back underground—frightened by my impressive power of flight, no doubt—" Bismark beamed, "—but if they ever show their eight-eyed faces again...by my flaps—I'll punt them straight to the moon!" Bismark reeled back his small leg and kicked. "Turn them into *real* star creatures," he snarled.

188

"No," the defeated aye-aye said, rising to her feet at last. "You can't do that. It's not their fault," she sputtered. "They're...they're innocent." Iris took a deep breath. "They didn't know what they were doing when they poisoned those pomelos. Some of them had never even been above ground until the star-stone rattled the earth!"

The aye-aye lowered her gaze. "It's Aye-Aye Iris ... she took advantage," she whispered. "Once the scorpions realized the harm they had caused, they wanted to fix it. They wanted to cure the sick animals. So they asked Aye-Aye Iris what to do. And she...." Iris paused and nervously twirled her long fur. "She told them that the only way to undo their damage was to bring her all the blue flowers. And then when you went after the flowers, too... well, it was perfect. Aye-Aye Iris told them that *you* were the evil ones. That *you* didn't want the sick animals to have the cure. That *you* were trying to steal the flowers." Iris bowed her head in shame.

Dawn, Tobin, and Bismark stood silent with shock.

"But...but..." Bismark sputtered. "But they were about to sting me! They were about to sting my lovely Dawn!"

"Iris knows, she knows!" wailed the aye-aye,

suddenly bursting into tears. "She told them to strike! They thought you were evil. They would have never tried to hurt you if Iris didn't tell them to." The aye-aye's long-fingered hands rose up to cover her face.

"Oh my." Tobin sighed. "Is that really true? Those poor scorpions are innocent?"

"Visitors in an unfamiliar land," murmured the fox. She shook her head side to side. "In a way, they really were *aliens*, weren't they?"

"*Mon dieu!*" Bismark took up his stick and waved it at the aye-aye again. "You sinister *señorita*! Taking advantage of those poor little glow-bulbs!"

Iris's body shook as the tears streamed down her face. "It's true! It's true!" she sobbed. "But this was the only way Iris could earn everyone's trust!" She turned to the other creatures. "It would've worked, right? All the animals that were never nice to Iris—once she had the cure, everyone would talk to her! Be kind to her. You would have been…you would have been her friends!"

The lemurs shifted uneasily.

"Gosh, Iris," one of them whispered. "We never thought of it that way."

"By all that glides, how could anyone be so insecure?" Bismark cried. The sugar glider looked sideways at the meteor's shiny surface. Catching a glimpse of his reflection, he quickly smoothed some hair over his bald spot. Then he cleared his throat and continued. "As I was saying," he went on, "if you want to be loved, all you have to do is be yourself! Besides, with a little trim, a long bath, and a friendly smile, you wouldn't make such a scary *amiga* at all."

The aye-aye blinked. "Really?" she asked.

Tobin nodded and smiled.

"You mean…" Iris took a step forward. "You don't think my fur is foul?"

"No," said the fox. "Not at all."

Iris scratched her head. "You don't think my teeth are appalling?"

"Of course not!" responded the pangolin.

Iris looked down at her hands. "You're not repulsed by my long fingers?" she asked.

"Whoa, whoa, whoa." The sugar glider held up a flap. "Let's not get carried away now. One step at a time, my little *cucaracha*."

Dawn smiled. "It's okay to be different, Iris. In fact, it's good." The fox turned toward the lemurs. "It's our differences that make us unique. They define who we are."

"*Oui*! And besides, *muchacha*, everyone is a little strange! Take my smelly *amigo*, here," said Bismark, throwing a flap around Tobin. "Tell me, do you know anyone who can toot like my scaly friend?"

"And what about the scorpions?" The pangolin smiled. "They live underground, they have those dreadful claws, and they *glow* in the moonlight! That might seem strange to some."

"Yes," Dawn agreed, "I suppose we're all a little bit strange."

"Well *si*," said Bismark, "except for *moi*, of course. I'm just strangely attractive." Bismark gazed back into the meteor and admired his reflection with a crooked grin.

Tobin giggled. Dawn laughed. Even the aye-aye chuckled.

Suddenly, the early morning seemed to brighten with a remarkable light. "Look!" cried Tobin. "Another shooting star!"

"*Mon dieu*! Hey, *pangolino*, try not to say your wish aloud this time!" Bismark said. "Even if we all know what you're thinking. More pomelos for all, *correctomundo*?"

Tobin's mouth curled in a bashful smile, remembering his first wish on the fallen star.

"But this time, it will come true," Dawn said. "The trees will grow more pomelos. And when they fall, we'll plant their seeds here, where the scorpions made their mounds. Before long, this crater will be a new grove."

The fox nudged one of the clods beneath her feet—and it nudged back. All around, new, small mounds started to form. The scorpions were returning, digging their way to the surface. Rising to join the other nocturnals.

Dawn gave a friendly nod to the eight-eyed creatures as they poked their heads above ground. Then she turned to Iris.

The aye-aye was looking up, the early morning light filling her face, reflecting her newfound hope. The pangolin placed a gentle claw on her back. Bismark wrapped a flap around Tobin.

"Yes," said Dawn, "we'll plant a new grove— one fresher and richer than any other." The fox surveyed the animals around her—all different, but all at peace. Her face relaxed in a serene smile. "And *everyone*," she continued, "no matter how odd their fingers, how strange their claws, or how numerous their eyes—will always be welcome."

Read All Three
Nocturnal Adventures!

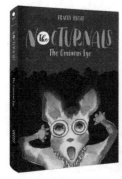

Visit nocturnalsworld.com
to watch animated videos, download fun nighttime
activities and check out a map of the Brigade's
adventure at nocturnalsworld.com/map/

*

Teachers and Librarians get Common Core Language Arts
and Next Generation Science guides for the book series.

*

#NocturnalsWorld

Acknowledgements

Just as the beauty and humor of Dawn, Tobin, and Bismark reside in the nature of friendship and collaboration, so too does the joy of bringing their stories to life.

These qualities begin with Tracey Hecht, who has created a world both in The Nocturnals and at Fabled Films Press that is a wonder to inhabit. Tracey, as a mentor and friend, you have taught me more about the art of storytelling and the ways of life than should have been possible in one short year. I hope we share many more together, both creatively and beyond.

This book would not exist without my other colleagues in the writer's room, Tommy Fagin and Sarah Fieber. Tommy, thank you for breaking me into this work with a steady stream of friendliness, counsel, and wit. Sarah, you have been a true friend, and you took The Fallen Star to the finish line with your leadership, guidance, and contributions when they were needed most.

Susan Lurie, our indefatigable editor, working with you is an honor; you constantly amaze me with your eye for narrative and your ability to push our team to new heights. Kate Liebman, our amazing illustrator, you turn our stories into the immersive adventures we strive for them to be.

The team behind The Nocturnals extends throughout all of Fabled as well. Stacey Ashton, if anyone is reading these words, you are a main reason why; likewise, thank you Michele Garza, Joe Gervasi, Lisette Farah, Jerry Li, Wiley Saichek, Erin Szczechowski, and Nicole Wheeler for all you do to connect us with our readers. Thanks also to Bailey Carr, Waymond Singleton, and the team at SJI, who animate these stories in their respective and respectively brilliant ways.

Finally, I'd like to briefly mention a creative team just beyond the one at Fabled: Asa, Brian, Daniel, Ian, and Lydia, you have lived with The Nocturnals just as much as I have, and the night world is better and richer with you in it. Finally, thank you to my grandmother, mother, and sister, the three women to whom this book is dedicated.

Thank you.

About the Author

Tracey Hecht is a writer and entrepreneur who has written, directed and produced for film. She has created a Nocturnals Read Aloud Writing program for middle graders in partnership with the New York Public Library that has expanded nationwide. She splits her time between Oquossoc, Maine and New York City.

About the Illustrator

Kate Liebman is an artist who lives and works in New York City. She graduated from Yale University, contributes to the Brooklyn Rail, and has shown her work at multiple galleries. She grew up in Santa Monica, California.

About Fabled Films

Fabled Films is a publishing and entertainment company creating original content for middle grade and Y/A audiences. Fabled Films Press combines strong literary properties with high quality production values to connect books with generations of parents and their children. Each property is supported with additional content in the form of animated web series and social media as well as websites featuring activities for children, parents, bookstores, educators and librarians.

FABLED FILMS PRESS
NEW YORK CITY

www.fabledfilms.com